THE
SECRET
IDENTITY
OF
DEVON
DELANEY

THE
SECRET
IDENTITY
OF
DEVON
DELANEY

By Lauren Barnholdt

mix

ALADDIN MIX

NEW YORK   LONDON   TORONTO   SYDNEY

m!x

ALADDIN MIX

An imprint of Simon & Schuster Children's Publishing Division

1230 Avenue of the Americas, New York, NY 10020

Copyright © 2007 by Lauren Barnholdt

All rights reserved, including the right of reproduction

in whole or in part in any form.

ALADDIN PAPERBACKS and related logo are registered

trademarks of Simon & Schuster, Inc.

ALADDIN MIX is a trademark of Simon & Schuster, Inc.

Designed by Tom Daly

The text of this book was set in Arrus.

Manufactured in the United States of America

First Aladdin Mix edition April 2007

10 9 8 7 6 5 4 3 2 1

Library of Congress Control Number 2007920235

ISBN-13: 978-1-4169-3503-2

ISBN-10: 1-4169-3503-7

For my sister, Krissi,
who always wanted to stay up late reading

Thank you so, so, much to:

My fab agent, **Nadia Cornier**, who didn't laugh when I told her I wanted to write a tween book. My editor, **Molly McGuire**, for taking over with such enthusiasm, and for her wonderful insight on how to make this book better. **Jennifer Klonsky**, for making things happen so fast, and for loving Devon as much as I do.

My **mom**, for always believing I was going to be a writer. My sister, **Kelsey**, for making my book signings very interesting. My **dad**, my **grandparents**, and my whole extended **family**, for such wonderful support.

Kiersten Loerzel, for having to deal with a few of my "secret identities" while we were growing up. **Kevin Cregg**, for being a wonderful friend. **Robyn Schneider**, for always letting me vent. **Rob Kean**, for putting up with my craziness on a daily basis.

Abby McDonald and **Scott Neumyer**, for being wonderful IM buddies.

And, of course, **Aaron Gorvine**, for being so amazing, and for letting me write most of this book at his house.

chapter **one**

Of course I've lied before. I mean, who hasn't? But they were small lies. White lies. Lies that wouldn't hurt anyone, and that no one even really *knew* were lies. Like when I told my friend Nicole last year at the sixth-grade dance that no one could see her underwear through her dress, even though everyone totally could, especially when the revolving lights passed over where we were standing. (By then, Nicole's mom had already dropped us off and gone home, so unless Nicole wanted to change into her gym clothes or find someone who had an extra, non-underwear-exposing dress hanging around, there was nothing anyone could do about it.)

Or when I tell my grandma that her spaghetti sauce is the best I've ever tasted, even though I like the sauce they use at Bertucci's way better.

Or the time my mom asked if I was feeding tuna to the cat, and I told her I wasn't, even though I was. She couldn't figure out why he was gaining so much weight when he was on his lean kibble, but since the vet said he's perfectly healthy, I figured giving him tuna wasn't a big deal.

But like I said, these are small lies. Minuscule, even. Not life-changing. And besides, I don't make it a point to lie all the time. Until last summer, of course, when I somehow became the biggest liar in Connecticut, creating a total made-up life that had nothing to do with my real life at all.

My mom says that karma always comes around to get you, and I guess it's true. Because last summer I was a total liar, and now, right here, in the middle of Mr. Pritchard's third-period math class, my whole world is about to come crashing down. Mr. Pritchard is at the front of the classroom, and standing next to him is Lexi Cortland, which pretty much means that my life is over. Because Lexi knows I'm a liar. Actually, no, she doesn't know I'm a liar, she's the one I lied *to*, and now she's here and it's going to become apparent that I'm a liar because—

"Devi!" Lexi squeals, right in the middle of Mr. Pritchard introducing her to the class.

Mr. Pritchard looks around, and I slink down in my seat. "Oh." Mr. Pritchard sounds surprised. "Alexis, do you know Devon Delaney?"

"Yes!" Lexi says. "We only spent the whole summer together!"

"Great," says Mr. Pritchard. "Why don't you take the seat next to her? It always helps to see a familiar face."

Lexi beams and makes her way down the aisle toward me. She's wearing a silver skirt and a beaded pink tank top with a short, fitted jacket over it. Her nails match her lip gloss.

"Devi!" Lexi says. It sounds weird having her call me that, since everyone else at school calls me Devon.

"Hey," I say, wondering if I should pretend I don't know her. I could make her think she was mistaking me for someone she *thought* she knew, like the time I thought I saw this girl from my church in the cafeteria but it turned out it wasn't her. And the girl was all "I'm not Beth." And I was like, "Oh, okay, sorry." It wasn't a big deal. Maybe I can just pretend I'm not Devon. I practice looking confused.

"Oh, hi." I squint at her like I don't know who she is.

"Can you believe I'm here?" she says. Mr. Pritchard drones on up front, not even caring that she's talking. Teachers always let new people get away with everything. "I wanted to tell you I was transferring, I'm so sorry I didn't, but I thought it would be fab if it was a surprise!"

Yeah. Really fab.

"Mmm," I say, still trying to pretend like I don't know her. I figure that eventually, if I keep this up, she'll just be like, "What's wrong? Aren't you Devon?" And I'll be like, "Yes, I'm Devon, but I've never seen you before." And she'll be like, "Oh, okay, sorry, wrong Devon." And that will be that. Although Lexi does know my last name. But I could try to keep that secret for a while. Maybe.

"Devi, I'm so glad you're here," she says, grabbing my arm. "I've had the most horrible morning. I don't know anyone, and I was totally afraid I'd have to sit alone at lunch. I've been looking for you all over, but every time I asked someone about you, they acted like they had no idea who you were."

"Mmm," I say again.

"Devi, what's wrong with you?" she says, looking at

me with wide eyes. "Are you sick or something? You're being weird." She takes in the jeans and pink UConn hoodie I'm wearing. When Lexi and I spent the summer together, I never wore jeans. I wore lots of skirts, lots of cute shorts, and lots of tank tops. I always had my hair perfectly straightened, and I wore tons of lip gloss. "Seriously, are you okay?" Lexi asks again, frowning. "Oh my God!" she says, her eyes brightening. "You're wearing the bracelet!" She looks down at my wrist, and there's the purple and gold beaded bracelet we made before I left. We went to the store together to pick out the beads and spent a whole afternoon working out the perfect color combinations before stringing them together. Lexi holds up her wrist and shows me the matching bracelet.

So much for pretending to be someone else.

"Yeah," I say, "I'm wearing it." I look ahead, hoping she gets the message. The message being, you know, to be quiet.

"Oh, Devi, this is going to be such a good year!" she says. "I'm so glad I know you, I mean, how lucky am I? Knowing one of the most popular girls at my new school before I even start?" She squeals. Mr. Pritchard ignores her. What is the deal with him, anyway? Why is it teachers are always enforcing the rules when you don't want them to? And now, when a girl who has the ability to ruin your life shows up prattling away about nonsense, they don't? They just keep going on and on about the value of pi.

"So we'll sit together at lunch, right? Thank God!" She smiles, revealing a mouthful of braces. "And I can't wait to meet Jared!"

Mr. Pritchard picks that moment to tell us to quiet down, and Lexi smiles and rolls her eyes at me. "Meet me outside the cafeteria before lunch," she says, then turns and faces the front of the classroom.

I try not to throw up. Because Lexi Cortland thinks I'm dating Jared Bentley. Jared Bentley, who is the hottest guy I've ever seen. Jared Bentley, who plays soccer but is also on the seventh-grade student council, which is totally contradictory. Jared Bentley, who doesn't even know I'm alive.

This whole thing is my parents' fault. If they hadn't gone uber-psycho and decided they needed time to work out their problems (or as my mom likes to call them, "marital challenges and roadblocks"), I never would have been sent to live with my grandmother for the summer. And I never would have met Lexi Cortland. Which means I never would have lied about

Jared Bentley being my boyfriend, or that I was one of the most popular girls in my school.

Don't get me wrong, I'm glad my parents stayed together. Although it *is* kind of annoying to see them kissing each other when I walk into the family room, or whenever they think my little sister, Katie, and I aren't looking. But why couldn't they have stayed together with us around? Why did they have to ship us ninety miles away for the summer?

I spend all of my fourth-period earth science class silently cursing my parents, and when the bell rings signaling the beginning of lunch, I consider just skipping it and hanging out in the library. I could get my best friend, Melissa, to come with me. And then I can just avoid this whole thing. Until I come up with some sort of brilliant plan that will allow me to save myself, before everyone finds out I lied about Jared Bentley being my boyfriend and I get completely humiliated and become the outcast of Robert Hawk Junior High.

I rush to the caf, hoping Melissa hasn't bought her hot lunch yet so I can whisk her off to the library for a quick, secret conference. But as soon as I get there, Lexi Cortland screams my name from the popular kids' table in the corner. "DEVI!" she yells, standing up and waving. "Come on! I saved you a seat!"

Crap. Now what am I supposed to do? I can't very well go sit at Jared Bentley's table. That would be disastrous. I mean, Lexi thinks he's my boyfriend, and how can I explain that one? Why and how is Lexi sitting at the popular kids' table, anyway? It's her first day of school! The A-list is so not that easy to penetrate.

I ignore Lexi and walk toward the corner where Melissa is sitting.

"Hey, Mel," I say, grabbing her and lifting her out of her chair. Seriously, I did. Lift her, I mean. Melissa is the smallest girl in our class. Which causes certain problems because she still has to buy clothes in the kids department, and also because at the beginning of the past two school years, her teachers have expressed concern over her size and have sent her to the guidance counselor, who then calls her parents in. And Mel's parents have to explain to them that, no, Melissa doesn't have an eating disorder, she eats tons (she does too—one time she ate a whole Domino's Pizza at a sleepover and was still hungry), and thank you for your concern, but no, they are not in denial, and please don't call them down to the school anymore for this, because they have jobs and it interrupts their workday and also upsets Mel.

"What are you doing?" Mel asks.

"I'll explain in a second," I hiss, hoarding her toward the door.

"I'm eating lunch!" she protests, her blue eyes crinkling as she frowns at me. She glances back at her lunch tray.

"You can have mine," I say, thrusting my brown-bag lunch at her.

"But I don't want yours," she protests. "I want the pizza that's on my tray. What are you—"

"No time to explain!" I say, moving faster. I step on Gregory Weston's foot as I try to make my way through the throng of kids in the cafeteria.

"Watch it!" he says.

"Sorry," I yell over my shoulder. I'm four feet from the door when suddenly, the jig is up.

"Devi!" Lexi screams, grabbing my shoulder. Her perfectly manicured nails exert slight pressure into my skin. "I was looking for you! I'm sitting at your table, can you believe it? Come on, I saved you a seat."

"Oh, I can't," I say, brushing my hair away from my face and trying to shield Mel from Lexi, all the while moving us toward the door. "Mel and I are going to the library and—"

"Oh, is this Melissa?" Lexi squeals. She jumps up and down, her wristful of bracelets jangling as she does so. "I've heard so much about you!"

Melissa frowns at Lexi. "Who are you?" she asks, looking between me and Lexi, confused. The thing is, I never mentioned Lexi or the other girls I hung out with this summer to Mel. I know it sounds horrible, but I told Mel my summer consisted of sitting around at Gram's with my little sister, watching lots of reality TV (*Dancing with the Stars* was my favorite), and reading lots of books. It worked until Mel asked which books I had read, and in reality, I'd only read two books while at Gram's, one of them a Harlequin romance I'd found behind the bed in the guest room, and which, surprisingly, made me want to read others. (Even though I had to hide the cover from my sister, Katie, by reading it under the blankets with a flashlight after she'd fallen asleep. I really didn't think Katie should be exposed to such, um, rippling muscles. Although at one point, I was very tempted to show her, because I really couldn't figure out if the muscles on the cover model were real or added with Photoshop. But I controlled myself.) Anyway, I couldn't really tell Mel I had read a Harlequin, so I started making up books, and then she asked me what I'd thought about some of them because, unlike me, apparently Mel really *had* spent her summer reading. It was almost a problem, but I changed the subject by bringing up the fact that I'd heard Brent Madison (her crush) was going to be in advanced math this year, which was the same class Mel was in. I had to sit through half an hour of her wondering what she should do about this problem (i.e, find a seat next to him or not, because if she sat next to him, it would help her get to know him, but if she didn't sit next to him, her grade would probably be better, and how could she risk her math grade for some guy?), but it was worth it.

"I'm Lexi!" Lexi says now. She grabs Mel in a hug. I look around, wondering if I'm perhaps on one of those hidden-camera shows. Like *Punk'd*, only for noncelebrities.

"Oh," Mel says, hugging Lexi back hesitantly. She gives her a few pats on the shoulder.

"Come sit!" Lexi says.

"Oh, no, we can't," I say, looking around nervously. "We're on our way to the library."

"The library!" Lexi says, throwing her head back and laughing. The lights of the cafeteria bounce off her braces. "Don't be silly, Devi." Mel's eyebrows shoot up at the use of the word "Devi." "Come sit with me! I'm at Jared's table." Mel's eyebrows shoot up even more.

"But how did—" I start.

"I couldn't find you," Lexi says, tossing her long blond hair over her shoulder. "So when I got to the cafeteria, I asked a girl where Jared Bentley was sitting, because I figured that's where you'd be. I thought you said in math you were going to meet me outside the cafeteria at the beginning of lunch."

"I, uh, forgot," I say lamely. Mel's eyes are now practically bugging out of her head, and I send her a silent message not to say anything that could potentially ruin my life.

"Come on," Lexi says. "We're missing lunch. And that guy is totally staring at me." She looks in distaste at the table next to us, where Mark Gibson's eyes are almost as big as Mel's. You can't blame him. Lexi is wearing a very short skirt.

"Lexi," I say, taking a deep breath. "I really can't."

"Why not?" Lexi says, her eyes narrowing. She looks at me suspiciously. "What's the problem?" This is the moment of truth. This is the time where I should come clean, I should tell Lexi that everything I told her this summer was completely made up, that Jared Bentley and I are not dating, that no one calls me "Devi," and that I don't usually look the way I did this summer.

"Lexi, I—"

"Alexis Cortland!" a voice booms suddenly. I turn

around to see one of the guidance counselors, Mr. Boone, standing behind us. Mr. Boone is really cool. He totally saved the seventh grade a couple of weeks ago when the eighth graders tried to fix the Robert Hawk Junior High penny contest for the Make-A-Wish Foundation.

"Mr. Boone," Lexi says sweetly. "What are you doing here?"

"I'm looking for *you*," Mr. Boone says. He adjusts his navy blue striped tie. Mr. Boone is always adjusting his tie. I don't know why. Other than the fact that maybe his tie is always loose? Or maybe he feels uncomfortable all dressed up, like the hero in one of the romance novels I read this summer. He was a carpenter (the guy in the book, not Mr. Boone) and he fell in love with this woman who had a lot of money. She was an heiress or something, and he was doing work on her house. Anyway, she took him to this huge event, kind of like a ball, and he had to wear a tuxedo, and he was very uncomfortable. Because he was used to going around shirtless all the time (to show off his rippling muscles, I think, which is why the heiress got interested in him in the first place). I imagine Mr. Boone walking around with no shirt on, and I blush.

"Why were you looking for me?" Lexi asks.

"Because you were supposed to spend your lunch period in my office, going over your schedule for this year," Mr. Boone says. He adjusts his tie again.

"I totally forgot," Lexi says in a tone that makes me think she totally did not. "Let me just get my stuff and I'll meet you in guidance." She turns to me. "I'll IM you later, okay, Devi?" She blows me a kiss and turns on her heel to grab her stuff. Mr. Boone follows her, presumably so she doesn't "forget" again.

Suddenly, my head is spinning and I collapse into the nearest chair.

Mel's eyes are still the size of saucers. "Um, you want to tell me what's going on?" she asks, plopping down in the chair next to me. "Devi?"

chapter two

I spend the next half hour in the library with Mel, filling her in on the Lexi debacle. We then make the following list:

Lies, Realities, and Possible Solutions

    Lie Number One: I am popular.

    Reality: I am not.

    Possible Solution: Somehow become popular? (At this point, Mel points out that if I knew how to do this, I would already have done it.)

    Why This Solution Won't Work: See above comment by Mel.

Lie Number Two: I am dating Jared Bentley.

Reality: Jared Bentley doesn't know my name. I don't think. One time earlier this year, he asked me if he could borrow a writing utensil in English. And all I had was this pen my grandmother had given me over the summer that was purple and said DEVON in huge yellow letters. Maybe he remembers this?

Possible Solution: Get Jared Bentley to go out with me.

Why This Solution Won't Work: Jared Bentley is tall, blond, and quite amazing. Every single girl in our junior high has a crush on him (even some of the eighth graders), so it's unlikely he would want to go out with me.

Possible Solution: Tell Lexi that Jared and I broke up.

Why This Solution Won't Work: The thing is, even though this is the first time I've *seen* Lexi, we still IM sometimes. And the last time we talked was last night, when Lexi told me she had this huge surprise for me. ("Who does that?" Mel asks at this point. "Just shows up at someone's school and doesn't tell them? And you have a secret IM friend?" She looks shocked, like she can't believe I'm having some sort of weird, behind-her-back IM conversations.) Anyway, I can't tell Lexi that Jared and I broke up, because last night, I was acting like Jared and I were still together. And what if she's all, "That's funny, last night you two were still going out, you PROBABLY MADE THE WHOLE THING UP AND ARE NOW STAGING A BREAKUP SO THAT NO ONE THINKS YOU'RE PSYCHO."

Lie Number Three: I'm always dressed like a fashionista. Although if you want to get technical, this one isn't really a lie. It's more of a misconception, since I never actually *told* Lexi that I always dressed the way I did this summer. She just sort of assumed I was perpetually dressed in cute outfits. In reality, I'm more of a jeans-and-hoodies kind of girl. I'm not a slob or anything, I'm just not dressed up all the time.

Possible Solution: Start dressing like a fashionista again.

Why This Solution Won't Work: The only reason I was able to dress like a fashionista in the first place was because my parents were feeling uber-guilty about sending me off to my grandma's for the summer, so they were, um, quite liberal with their cash. My dad even gave me his credit card number so I could shop online. Now that they're back together, I'm lucky if I see my allowance. And all the cute clothes I bought over the summer were *summer* clothes. And now it's October. I mean, how can I show up at school wearing tank tops and sandals? I'd look like a freak. A cute freak. But a freak.

Possible Solution: Tell Lexi I've developed some sort of rare skin disease that causes me to be allergic to designer clothes. Also let her know that this disorder may be catching, so she might want to stay away from me unless she is prepared to give up her Prada and BCBG.

Why This Solution Won't Work: Lexi Cortland is not stupid.

BOTTOM LINE: I AM IN DEEP TROUBLE.

When I get home from school, my mom's at the kitchen table, on her laptop. She's a freelance Web designer now, which is one of the things she and my dad agreed on this summer. Apparently my mom was feeling suffocated by her job at the design firm where she worked and she wanted to start her own business, but my dad was worried that if she did, we'd all be out on the street, homeless and with no food. Which even *I* thought was kind of ridiculous, because my dad is a pharmaceutical rep, and so is Darcy Marino's, this girl in my math class. Darcy's parents have four kids, and her mom stays at home and takes care of them. Their house is bigger than ours, and I don't think Darcy or her brothers ever went hungry or anything.

Anyway, my mom thought that since my dad worried we were all going to end up homeless, that meant he didn't believe in her abilities and wasn't encouraging her to pursue her dreams. So she got really mad, which led to the "rifts and tension" in their marriage. But ever since Katie and I got back from my grandma's, my dad has seemed super supportive. I think it's because they're going to a marriage counselor, and it seems to be helping. (FYI: My mom and dad make up excuses when they go to their counseling appointments, but I totally found the brochure in my mom's desk once while I was looking for a red Sharpie to use for my social studies poster on Communist Russia. It's kind of ridiculous to keep it a secret, if you ask me, because I'm thirteen and I wouldn't freak out about it or anything. But I do my best not to let on that I know, and also to keep it a secret from Katie, because I don't want anyone getting upset.)

"Hey, honey," my mom says, standing up and stretching. "How was school?"

"Good," I lie, figuring it's best not to say anything about the whole my-life-possibly-being-ruined thing. I open the cupboard and pull down a box of peanut butter and chocolate chip granola bars.

"Hello," Katie says, walking into the room. She's wearing a bathing suit and a pair of ice skates.

"Oh, honey," my mom says, "you shouldn't wear your skates in the house."

"Why not?" Katie asks. "I'm in training."

"Well," my mom says slowly, "that's great, but you need to wear your blade guards if you're going to be walking around like that."

Katie is five, and thinks she's an Olympian. Or, going to be an Olympian. The problem is, she wants to get to the Olympics, but can't decide what she wants to go to the Olympics *for*. So one week she's an ice-skater, the next she's a gymnast, etc. One time she came to the dinner table wearing a tutu she had left over from ballet lessons she took when she was three. (It was way too small for her, and also confusing to everyone, because ballet isn't an Olympic sport. When we told her this, she burst into tears, because ballet was her "one true shot at the gold.")

Katie can be quite dramatic.

"Mom, wearing my blade guards does not help when I am out on the ice, trying to stay balanced."

"You need to wear your blade guards," my mom

repeats firmly. "Otherwise you're going to ruin the floor, and we'll have to spend the money we're currently using for your skating lessons to pay for a new one."

Katie crosses her arms and puts a pained expression on her face. Katie is having what my grandmother calls "a difficult transition." Basically, since my parents pretty much gave her whatever she wanted over the summer (a new bike, new skates, a balance beam so she could practice being an Olympic gymnast, and a trampoline), and my grandmother never made her do anything around the house, she's not used to people saying no to her. Which is why she pitches a lot of fits.

"I want some juice," she says now.

"Fine," my mom says, pushing her hair away from her face and standing up from the table. She's wearing blue yoga pants and a pink long-sleeved fleece shirt. Now that my mom works from home, she wears this kind of stuff a lot. She stops for a minute, considering my sister's request. "Katie, honey, you can get the juice yourself. Mommy's working." She sits back down at her computer, looking satisfied.

Katie rolls her eyes and makes a big production of sliding her ice-skate blades across the kitchen floor. I'm pretty sure that one of the things my mom is working on in therapy has to do with not letting her guilt get

the best of her, which might cause her to let me and Katie get spoiled. Which means this is probably not the best time to ask her if I can go away to boarding school, since my life is a huge mess.

"Devon," my mom says. "Listen, your father and I are going out tonight, so you're going to have to watch Katie."

"No, thanks," Katie says, pulling a container of orange juice out of the refrigerator. She totters on her skates over to the counter. "I don't want Devon to watch me."

I reach up into the cupboard and pull down a pink plastic cup and set it on the counter for her. "It'll be fun, Katie," I say.

"How come?" she asks.

"It just will," I say, hoping she'll accept that. Katie gets a little weird when she has to stay home alone with me. It has to do with what happened this summer. She thinks that when my parents leave, they're going to be gone for a really long time.

Katie sighs and starts pouring the juice carefully into her cup.

"How long do I have to babysit for?" I ask my mom, not really caring. Babysitting for Katie isn't hard. Especially since my mom just bought her *Miracle*, the true story of the U.S. Olympic hockey team on DVD. Katie has been watching it over and over and over.

"Just a few hours," my mom says. "We're going out to dinner."

The phone rings, and I lunge for the cordless.

"Hello?" I say, without checking the caller ID.

"Devi? It's Lexi."

"Oh, um, hi," I say, wandering into my room. I throw myself down on the bed, wondering why Lexi is calling me. I gave her my phone number at the end of the summer, but until this point, our contact has been contained to instant message conversations.

"You weren't online," Lexi says. She sounds accusatory, like I've done something horrible.

"Sorry," I say, "I just got home." I look down at my bed and pull at a stray thread that's popped out of the lining of my comforter.

"So check it," Lexi says. "I was thinking we could go together tonight."

"Get together?" I ask.

"No, *go* together," Lexi says, sounding slightly exasperated. "To the mall? With Jared and Kim and everyone?"

It takes me half a second to realize that she's talking about some A-list get-together that's planned for tonight, and since she thinks I'm dating Jared, she just assumes I'm invited. Which I'm not.

"Listen, Lexi—"

"My mom can drive if your mom can pick us up," Lexi says matter-of-factly.

"I can't," I say. "I have to babysit for Katie." Which isn't a lie. I do have to babysit for Katie. Besides, even if I didn't have to babysit for Katie, I couldn't just show up at the mall to some A-list meet-up. Especially with Lexi. Especially when she thinks I'm dating Jared Bentley. "Hey, wait," I say, confused. "How did you get invited?"

"After I finished with Mr. Boone, I went back to the cafeteria," Lexi says. "Kim invited me." Kim is Kim Cavalli, who's one of the most popular girls in the seventh grade. Unreal. Girls spend their lives trying to be friends with Kim. Lexi's here for a day and she's already hanging out with her.

"Listen," I say, deciding now is the time to tell Lexi the truth. But what do I say, exactly?

Choice A: Lexi, I'm not popular, I'm a total liar, Jared Bentley doesn't even know I'm alive.

Choice B: Gotta go, Lexi, talk to you, erhm, never. (Then avoid Lexi at school forever.)

Choice C: Lexi, I have to confess something. You

see, I'm really not going out with Jared, and I'm really not that popular. I don't know why I told you all that stuff this summer, and I'm really sorry. I didn't mean to lie to you.

Choice B seems like the most logical solution, but the problem (besides, of course, the fact that I could end up a social outcast), is that I really *do* want to be friends with Lexi. We had a lot of fun together over the summer, and we talked a lot about the stuff that was going on with my parents. Which was nice, because nobody else knows my parents were thinking about getting divorced. Not even Mel. It would be horrible if Lexi hated me.

Suddenly, something takes over my body. It's like I'm not myself, but someone else. Some other Devon. One who has no idea what she's doing. I say, "Listen, Lexi, it's really important that you don't say anything to anyone about me and Jared dating."

"How come?" Lexi says, and I think if she had sounded suspicious at all, I probably wouldn't have been able to lie. But she sounds genuinely interested, and before I can stop myself, I say, "Because Mel has a crush on him, so our relationship is totally secret." Mel. Has. A. Crush. On. Him. And. So. Our. Relationship. Is. Totally. Secret. Oh my God. I have lost my mind. I've seriously gone crazy. It's even worse than the summer, because over the summer, it was crazy to pretend to be popular and everything, but at least that was kind of normal because what thirteen-year-old girl doesn't want to be popular? It was kind of like I was playing a role and—oh my God. I'm obviously a pathological liar. What is a pathological liar, exactly? Is it someone who lies, and then believes her lies? No, because if the person didn't *realize* she was lying, she wouldn't be a liar, she'd just be insane. And I definitely know I'm lying. Of course, I could also be insane.

"Mel?" Lexi says, sounding excited. "Your best friend, Mel?"

"Yes," I say, closing my eyes. I lie down on my bed. I wonder if I'm too young to get an ulcer from stress. My great-uncle Tony has a stress ulcer. But that's because his son, my mom's cousin Darren, moved his five children and wife into my great-uncle Tony's spare bedroom and won't leave. "Mel has a crush on Jared and, uh, she would kill me if she found out we were dating. So, ah, you can't tell anyone."

"Who knows?" Lexi asks.

"Um, just me and you," I say. "So you have to keep it a secret." I am a horrible person. Mel doesn't like Jared at all. In fact, she thinks he's totally ridiculous.

(This is mostly because one time when she was coming out of the girls' locker room after gym, someone opened the door to the boys' locker room at the same time, and she got to peek in. And what Mel saw was Jared Bentley, standing at the sink after gym, putting gel in his hair. And Mel thought that was really weird and very conceited, because they have gym seventh period, and there are only eight periods in the day, which means that Jared Bentley couldn't even go forty minutes without his hair looking perfect.)

"Oh, Devi, I won't!" she says. "I wish you would have told me about this earlier, though. I mean, I could have slipped at school today!"

"You didn't, though, right?" I say, my heart speeding up. "You didn't tell anyone about Jared and me?"

"I don't think so," Lexi says, considering.

"Well, that's good," I say, trying to sound breezy. "Listen, I'm probably going to break up with him soon, anyway. The guilt is killing me."

"Oh, Devi, you're such a good friend!" Lexi exclaims. "I mean, I'm sure Melissa is nice and everything, but . . ." She trails off, not wanting to say what she's thinking. Which is that while Mel is nice and cute enough, she's not in Jared Bentley's league. But then again, neither am I. Although . . . I sit up on my bed, starting to think. Why aren't I good enough for Jared? I mean, I had Lexi fooled this whole summer. I wore cute clothes and acted fun and confident, and she totally believed it. Lexi was way popular at her old school (unlike me, I'm sure she didn't make up all the stories she told me, including the one where she had three guys asking her to the sixth-grade Valentine's Day dance), and she was apparently getting in with the popular crowd here.

"Listen, I have to go," I say, my mind racing. I'm wondering:

♥ how long I have to pretend to have a secret relationship with Jared before I can have a fake breakup with him without looking obvious.

♥ if I should tell Mel she now has a crush on Jared, and wonder if she will then refuse to be my best friend anymore, causing me to be totally friendless and a complete outcast, since she will most likely tell everyone I made up the story about me dating Jared to get revenge.

♥ how I got myself into this mess in the first place.

"Okay," Lexi says, sounding disappointed. "I'll tell Jared you said hi when I see him at the mall."

"No!" I say, a little too sharply.

"Why not?" Lexi asks, sounding confused.

"I just told you," I say, trying not to get flustered, therefore making Lexi mad at me. That's another thing. Now I have to try to stay on Lexi's good side, because if she gets mad at me for some reason, she might tell my secret. This is all extremely complicated. "You have to keep it a secret. It's a secret relationship. No one knows." I emphasize the word "secret," hoping she gets how serious it is this time.

"But Jared already knows you two are going out," Lexi says, "so what's the big deal? I'll make sure no one hears. It will be like a secret between the three of us."

I bite my lip and try not to scream. I make my way over to my computer and check to see if Mel's online. "Lexi going to mall tonight with Jared, etc." I type "wants me 2 go, what do I do?"

"U go," Mel replies immediately, "otherwise, disaster. keep eye on them."

"Hello?" Lexi's saying on the phone. "Are you there, Devi? Are you talking on instant messenger?" she asks suspiciously.

"No," I say. "Of course not. Listen, Lexi, I think I'm going to be able to make it tonight after all."

"Fab!" Lexi says, and I imagine her bouncing up and down like she always does when she's happy. "My mom will pick you up at six."

chapter three

It takes a while to sell my parents on the idea of letting me take Katie out of the house. Actually, at first I tried to get my mom to let me not babysit at all and just go by myself, but she wasn't having it. She said it was because I "had already made a commitment" to her by saying I would watch my sister, but this really made no sense, because I had just made the commitment about fifteen minutes ago, so I didn't really think it should count.

My dad acted like it would be okay for me to go (although I think it was because he wanted to be able to skip therapy—I suspect my dad secretly believes that the therapy stuff is really unnecessary, and only does it to make my mom happy).

Anyway, we compromised, and my mom said I could bring Katie with me to the mall, and I couldn't decide if that was a good thing or not, because on the one hand it meant I got to go, but on the other hand, it meant Katie was going too, which was, you know, decidedly not cool. But what could I do? I couldn't risk Lexi and Jared being alone with each other.

So that's how I end up in the back of Lexi's mom's van, with Katie sitting next to me.

"So, what are you girls going to do at the mall?" Mrs. Cortland asks, glancing at Katie and me in the rearview mirror. Katie is wearing her too-small pink tutu over heavy blue tights. Apparently, it's her "skating warm-up" outfit. Normally, I would never have let her leave the house like that, but my parents had already left by the time Lexi's mom showed up and Katie wouldn't listen to me. I figured it was better to have an ice-skating-warm-up-outfit-clad Katie than a pitching-a-fit-and-screaming Katie. Besides, I have bigger problems, like:

(a) what the A-list is going to think when I show up at their gathering when I was:

(1) not invited

(2) accompanied by my little sister

(b) how I was going to convince Lexi that Jared and I were dating when Jared, Lexi, and I were all in the same place.

"We're meeting up with some people from school," Lexi says. She flips down the visor over the passenger seat and studies her reflection in the mirror. She smiles at herself, checks her braces for food, and then carefully applies more lip gloss.

"Boys?" Lexi's mom asks, sounding amused. I definitely didn't tell my mom that there would be boys at the mall. And if I had, she wouldn't have sounded amused. She would have asked me three million questions, about who these boys were and how I knew them. But Lexi's mom is very different from my mom. Lexi's mom wears lots of makeup, and matches her purse to her outfit. She also lets Lexi do pretty much whatever she wants. "Yes, Mom," Lexi says, sighing. She reaches into the small purple bag on her lap and pulls out a brush and starts dragging it through her hair in long strokes.

Katie pokes me in the arm. "I have to go to the bathroom," she says.

"Not now," I tell her. "You can go when we get to the mall."

Mrs. Cortland glances at us in mirror again, and I smile at her in what I hope is a reassuring manner.

"So, Devi, Lexi tells me your parents are busy tonight?" Lexi's mom asks. I think she's cranky that she had to drive us and pick us up. But my parents were going to counseling, so it wasn't like they were going to cancel just so they could drive me to the mall.

"Yes," I say seriously. "They had an extremely important meeting to go to." She looks skeptical. "For my dad's work," I lie. What is up with me and lying? I do it once and now I can't stop. Lying to Lexi's mom shouldn't count, though. Over the summer, whenever I was hanging out at Lexi's house, Mrs. Cortland would ask five million questions about why Katie and I were staying with my grandmother for the summer. I told her it was because Katie and I needed a vacation. I didn't think it was really her business, and besides, it was embarrassing. I think Lexi told her the truth, though, because later in the summer I heard Mrs. Cortland on the phone with one of her friends, talking about how she had no idea where my parents were and how she wouldn't be surprised if we ended up staying with my grandmother forever. Ever since then, Mrs.

Cortland always looks at me warily, like I'm from some kind of broken home. Which is kind of ironic, because this summer Lexi and I spent most of our time at my grandma's house. Lexi liked that there were always people around and that my grandma baked a lot of brownies. The few times we hung out at Lexi's, I could never relax because I was always afraid I was going to spill something all over her mom's white carpets. And even though Lexi's mom was home most of time, it didn't seem like she spent that much time with Lexi.

Katie pokes me again. "DEVON!"

"What's wrong?" Lexi's mom asks now, sounding alarmed. "Is she cold in that outfit?" She peers at us closely in the rearview mirror. "What *is* that outfit?"

"It's her skating warm-up," I say simply.

"Her what?" Lexi's mom frowns.

"She's a very talented figure skater," I say. "She's probably going to be in the Olympics, so it's important that she stays focused on her sport."

Katie beams.

"So, Lexi," I say, "you never told me what you're doing here." All the lying and scheming, coupled with the shock of Lexi showing up at my school had thrown me off, and I had never even asked her *why* she was at my school. Suddenly. To ruin my life.

"My dad got transferred," Lexi says, sighing. "And at first he was just going to commute the hour and a half, but then mom found out about this house that was going on the market, so we decided to move."

Lexi's mom is a real estate agent, which is very strange, because I thought the whole point of being a real estate agent was to show houses and get people to buy them. It seemed all Lexi's mom really did this summer was hang around the house and walk on her treadmill. When I asked Lexi if her mom's boss ever got mad that she didn't come to work, Lexi told me her mom didn't have a boss, that she owned her own company.

"Yes, we got a great deal on the house because we moved at the right time," Mrs. Cortland says. She runs her fingers through her short, highlighted hair. "Lexi, are you wearing the same thing you wore to school to the mall?"

"Yes," Lexi says. "Why?"

"You have so many clothes," Mrs. Cortland says. "I wish you would wear them. Besides, this is your new school. And you really should do everything you can to make a good impression." She glances at Lexi pointedly, as if to say that hanging out with me is definitely not the way to accomplish said good impression.

"Devon, I really, really—" Katie starts.

"It's okay, honey," Mrs. Cortland says. "We're here."

She lets us off in front of the ice-cream shop in the mall where we're supposed to meet everyone. I take a deep breath and step out of the car. Katie jumps down behind me, and some glitter falls off her tutu and onto the pavement.

"What is that?" I ask her.

"What's what?" she asks.

"What just fell off of your tutu?"

"Glitter," Katie says, shrugging.

"I know glitter," I say, sighing. "But why is it falling off your tutu?"

"This is not a tutu!" Katie says. "This is a SKATING WARM-UP!"

"Fine," I say. "Why is there glitter falling off your skating warm-up?"

"Because I put glitter on it before we left," she says, rolling her eyes at my obvious stupidity. "Skaters get half their score from artistic impression." This makes no sense, but Lexi is out of the car now, so I don't fight her on it.

"This is going to be so fab," Lexi says, linking her arm through mine. "Are you excited that you're going to be seeing Jared?"

"Totally," I say, although in reality, I want to throw up. At least I look cute, so if I have a moment of complete and total humiliation, I'll be sure to do it while looking good. I'm wearing a short white denim skirt that I have leftover from the summer, along with a red sweater I stole out of my mom's closet. I used my hair straightener for the first time in months, and I'm wearing blush and pink lip gloss. I'm not deluded or anything—I know I look cute, but there's no way people are going to think I'm someone else.

Lexi opens the door to the mall, and Katie and I follow her in. With every step I take, my dread grows. I have no plan other than to try to keep Lexi and Jared far, far away from each other.

"Ooh, there they are!" Lexi yells, spotting Jared, Kim Cavalli, and Luke Nichols sitting at one of the tables outside the ice-cream store.

Kim jumps up from where she's sitting and envelopes Lexi in a huge hug, which is kind of ridiculous. I mean, they just met.

"Devon!" Katie says, tugging on my sleeve. "I GOTTA GO NOW!"

"Just a minute, Katie," I say. Kim stares at me and my sister.

"Aww," Lexi says, leaning down toward Katie. "It's

okay, Katie. I'll take you to the bathroom." Lexi is an only child, so she's always been kind of fascinated with Katie. This is because she doesn't have to put up with Katie acting crazy on a regular basis. Lexi takes Katie's hand, straightens up, and looks at me. "Be right back." They disappear into the restaurant.

Kim's still staring at me.

"Uh, hi," I say brilliantly. Please don't ask me what I'm doing here, please don't ask me what I'm . . .

"So you're friends with Lexi?" she asks curiously, and I can tell what she's thinking: how someone like me is friends with someone as fab as Lexi.

"Yeah," I say, using my "Devi" voice. (FYI: My Devi voice utilizes this thing called "tonal audiation" or something, which is this speech pattern that makes everything you say sound kind of like a question. I got the idea of using it when Mel and I did a project on it last year in health class.) "We spent all summer together."

Kim nods. "You're in my English class, right?"

"I think so," I say, trying to look like I'm not quite sure, even though I've been hyperaware of her presence in English, because Jared is also in that class and I like to keep tabs on how much they seem to be interested in each other. (Jared and Kim have never dated, but it only makes sense that they would or should—I mean, they're the most popular boy and girl.)

"Come on," Kim says, and I follow her over to the table where Jared and Luke are sitting.

"Where's Lexi?" Jared asks, looking confused. I'm standing next to Kim, and he seems to be talking to the space between us, so I can't tell who he's talking to. I have a small but distinct window of opportunity, and somehow I find the courage to grab it.

"Uh, she just ran to the bathroom," I say, so flustered that I forget to use my Devi voice. "But she'll be back." I slide into the empty seat between Jared and Luke. Kim sits down across from us. "I'm Devi," I say, figuring I need to get it out of the way before Lexi comes back, just in case Luke or Jared don't know my name and/or are tempted to call me Devon.

"She went to the bathroom?" Jared asks, ignoring my introduction. "For what?"

What does he mean for what? To go to the bathroom, of course. Or to take Katie at least. But I can't say that. That's embarrassing. Plus, I'm about to lose it because I just realized that I am CLOSER TO JARED BENTLEY THAN I HAVE EVER BEEN IN MY LIFE. Add to that the fact that he's wearing a T-shirt, which means his BARE ARM IS RIGHT NEXT TO MINE.

"She took Devi's sister to the bathroom," Kim says,

rolling her eyes. She reaches over and plucks a menu from behind the napkin dispenser and runs her eyes up and down the ice-cream selections.

"Your sister?" Jared asks, looking at me with new interest. "How old is she?"

"Uh, my sister?" I repeat, still not using my Devi voice. I seem to have lost the voice somewhere. Although, since this is the first time I can remember Jared actually speaking to me, except for that time in English when he asked to borrow a pencil, which totally doesn't count, I can't really be blamed. The Devi voice takes a certain level of concentration.

"Jared, knock it off," Kim says, rolling her eyes. "She's a kid." She looks back down at the menu. "They never have any good low-carb flavors here."

"She's a kid?" Jared asks, not letting it go. "Why'd you bring a kid to the mall?" He looks surprised, like children under ten have never been allowed shopping before.

I take a deep breath and concentrate on being Devi. On doing the same stuff I did this summer. How hard can it be? I had Lexi fooled. "I totally got stuck baby-sitting," I say. "So I had to bring her. No way I was gonna be stuck in the house all night doing nothing." I look over my shoulder anxiously for Lexi and Katie.

Jared nods. Luke, who's on the other side of me, has said nothing so far. "Hey," I say, turning to him. "You're Luke, right? I'm Devi." It's best to make sure all my bases are covered and that everyone at this table knows I'm Devi, so that there's no confusion later. Even though my heart is beating about three million times a minute.

"Yeah, I know," Luke says. "You're in my social studies class." I try not to show my shock. Luke knows who I am? I don't have time to dwell on this development because at that moment, Lexi comes back to the table. Katie's trailing along behind her, practicing what she calls her "toe flip" but which, as far as I can tell, is really just Katie jumping into the air and twirling around in a circle.

"I'm back!" Lexi declares, plopping into the chair across from me. She looks at the menu Kim has spread out on the table in front of us. "Did you guys order yet?"

"I don't even want ice cream," Jared says, looking bored. "I want to get over to the arcade and try out the new Modcon Five game."

"I heard it was sweet," Luke says.

"You guys are so corny," Kim says, rolling her eyes.

"We're getting ice cream. I saved up all my carbs just for this."

"Come on, Kim," Jared teases. "You can play Dance Dance Revolution just like you love." He looks at Lexi. "She loves DDR, but she pretends she thinks it's lame."

"I do not!" Kim screeches. She reaches across the table and tries to hit Jared on the top of the baseball hat he's wearing, but he blocks her arm and they fake wrestle for a second. Lexi raises her eyebrows and shoots me a look across the table. I can tell what she's thinking: *Why is your boyfriend flirting with another girl right in front of you?*

Before I can think of an answer, Luke stands up. "Come on," he says. "We can get ice cream after, if you still want it." Kim rolls her eyes, but she gets up too.

As we walk to the arcade, Lexi pulls me behind the rest of the group. "So what's the deal with Kim and Jared?" she asks.

I swallow. "What do you mean?"

"Why was he flirting with her so bad?"

"Was he?" I ask. "I didn't notice." Then I realize that if Jared really were my boyfriend, I would be more upset, so I backtrack. "I mean, they're good friends and everything, and they're always around each other, so maybe I just don't—"

"Hey," Jared says, dropping back to where we are. "Are you going to play DDR?" It's obvious that he's talking to Lexi, but she's looking down at the ground for some reason (I think it's because she's wearing these completely ridiculous shoes, and so it's hard for her to walk—the heels are seriously five inches tall), so I make it out like he's talking to me.

"Of course," I say, acting like Jared should obviously know this. Since, you know, he's my boyfriend and all.

"Cool," Jared says. He smiles and heads back up to the rest of the group, where Luke and Kim are fighting over what time Kim's mom is supposed to pick them up.

"I hate these shoes," Lexi mumbles.

"Then why did you wear them?" Katie asks, twirling around us. I almost forgot she was there.

"Because they're hot, Katie-Kate," Lexi says.

"Lexi has a boyfriend, Lexi has a boyfriend!" Katie sings. More glitter falls out of her "warm-up" and onto the floor. Katie mistakenly thinks that if you get dressed up, use the word "hot," or hang out with boys, that means you have a boyfriend.

"I don't have a boyfriend," Lexi says.

"Lexi and Jared, sitting in a tree, K-I-S-S-I-N-G!" Katie sings.

Lexi looks horrified. "Oh, no, honey," she says. "I would never move in on Devi's boyfriend. I'm not that kind of friend."

Katie stops twirling and looks at me, interested. "Devon, you have a boyfriend?"

"Yes," Lexi says. "Jared is Devi's boyfriend."

"No, he isn't," I rush on, but it's too late.

"Devon and Jared, sitting in a tree, K-I-S-S-I-N-G!" Katie amends her song, but keeps up with the twirling. I look fearfully ahead, trying to gauge how much distance is between Katie's voice and Jared.

"Oh, Devi, I'm so sorry!" Lexi says. "Your family doesn't know?"

I'm about to start crying. Deep breaths. What would Devi do? "My mom would flip out if she knew Jared and I were together," I say, rolling my eyes. "She's way overprotective."

"That sucks," Lexi says, nodding. "I hope I didn't get you in trouble."

"Nah," I say, "Katie will forget about this by the time we get home." I'm not sure if that's true, but I have bigger problems right now, i.e., shutting Katie up before someone hears her song.

"Katie," I say sweetly. "Don't you want to play Skee-Ball or something?"

We've reached the arcade now, and Jared, Kim, and Luke are at the cash machine a few feet away, changing dollars into quarters.

Katie nods. I pull a bunch of bills out of my pocket and hand them to her. This trip is going to be expensive. With the babysitting money I'm getting tonight, I'll probably just about break even. Katie scampers off into the arcade.

"Come on, Jared," Kim says. "You have to DDR with me." She grabs his arm.

Lexi shoots me a "Why is she hitting on your boyfriend?" look.

"Maybe later," Jared says. "I want to check out the new Modcon game."

"Luke?" Kim asks, giving him a smile and a coy look. "You wanna DDR with me?" She leans toward him. I shoot Lexi a look as if to say, "See! She wasn't hitting on my boyfriend, she's just a flirt."

"Maybe later," Luke says, taking off after Jared.

This is going beautifully! Not only is the A-list not making a big deal about me being here, but now the boys are going to be in a completely different section of the arcade, and Katie will be busy playing Skee-Ball! I am so good at this! Seriously, if I had known it would be this easy to pull off a fake relationship, I wouldn't have been stressing so much earlier.

For the next hour, Lexi, Kim, and I play DDR while the boys check out Modcon Five. Luckily, the Skee-Ball game is right next to us, so I'm able to keep an eye on Katie. Kim turns out to be surprisingly cool, and the arcade is so loud that it's almost impossible to talk, so I don't have to worry about dodging any conversation bullets.

When it's time to leave, I have four quarters left over and I put them in the DDR machine on our way out.

"Sweet," Jared says, jumping up onto the game next to me. The music starts playing, and I'm so thrown off by the fact that I'm actually DDR'ing with Jared Bentley that I mix up some of the steps.

"Come on, Devi," Jared says. "You gotta clear this level."

This almost messes me up more, but I force myself to concentrate, and when Jared and I both clear the level, he hugs me, which makes Lexi smirk like she's in on some kind of secret. And it makes my face feel so hot that I'm afraid Lexi will notice how red I am.

By the time we walk out of the mall, I'm starting to think that maybe I can pull this off. All I have to do is mooch off of Lexi's newfound popularity for the next week or two, and then I can stage a breakup and forget this whole thing ever happened.

"Hey," Jared says to me, when we're all standing on the curb, waiting for our respective rides. "Can I talk to you for a minute?" He grabs the sleeve of my sweater, and I almost faint.

"Um, sure," I say, praying Katie doesn't chose this moment to break into another round of K-I-S-S-I-N-G. Thankfully, she's silent, holding Lexi's hand and playing with a small blue plastic pony she got by turning in her Skee-Ball tickets.

"Listen," Jared says, once we're a safe distance from the group. I can see Lexi over his shoulder, trying to see what's going on. "I have to ask you something."

"Sure," I say, trying not to become mesmerized by his blue eyes. Is it possible that Jared is in love with me already? That it took one night of hanging out for him to realize we're supposed to be together? This means I totally won't have to even make up any more lies! Because Jared and I will ACTUALLY BE TOGETHER.

Jared leans in close to me, and for a second, I think

he's going to kiss me. "Do you think Lexi likes me?" he whispers.

"What?" I ask, taking a step back.

"Lexi," he says. "Could you talk to her for me, find out if she likes me?"

"Why?" This is not happening.

Imagined Conversation:

Jared: Lexi, will you go out with me?

Lexi: Aren't you going out with Devi?

Jared: No, why would you think that?

Lexi: Because that's what she told me.

Jared: What a liar. Let's tell everyone in school and ruin her life.

"Because she's totally hot," Jared says now, smiling. He must mistake my shock and silence for agreement, because he pats me on the shoulder and says, "Thanks, Devi. You rock."

He heads back to where everyone else is standing, and it takes all my strength not to collapse onto the pavement. Things just got three hundred times more complicated.

chapter four

Okay. This is not that big of a deal. I'm standing by my locker at school the next morning, thinking about how people have figured out problems way worse than this one. Like the Cuban Missile Crisis, for example. The country was on the brink of nuclear disaster, and it all worked out. So there is definitely a solution to the ridiculousness that is now known as my life. I just have to figure out what it is.

"Ooh-la-la," Mel says when she sees me. I'm wearing a pair of cute jeans and a tank top with a beaded sweater over it. My hair has been blown straight, and I am wearing pink lip gloss. This is my new look. I have decided that I can take my old, cute summer wardrobe and update it a little to make it warmer. "Dressing up for the boyfriend, are we?"

"Not funny," I say. I grab my math book out of my locker, slam it shut, and look around nervously. If I'm going to pull this off, I'm going to have to stay on top of every situation. Which means knowing where Lexi and Jared are at all times. I have no idea where they are right now. I'm obviously off to a very bad start.

"Here," Mel says, handing me our BFF notebook. Our BFF notebook is a blank, pink-and-purple-bound book that we use to write notes to each other. We keep passing it back and forth. We've done this since the fifth grade, and we've gone through at least eight or nine notebooks. Mel must have written in it last night.

"Thanks," I say, sliding it into my bag. I feel like a fraud. How can I deserve to be part of our BFF notebook when I told Lexi that Mel likes Jared? I slide my finger along the top of the notebook, wondering how I'm going to tell Mel about her crush on Jared. Maybe I'll just die from guilt and no one will ever find out what a huge liar I am.

"So how did it go last night?" Mel asks. "You had your away message up all night, and I tried to call, but no one answered." A second wave of guilt starts to slide up inside me. Last night when I got home, I ended up on the phone with Lexi until ten o'clock, when my mom finally caught me and made me get off. I noticed Mel beeping in on the caller ID, but I didn't answer it. It wasn't that I didn't want to talk to her. It was just that I needed to do damage control. Well, as much as I could, anyway, given that the situation is a total disaster.

"It went . . . okay," I say slowly. "Except for the fact that Jared told me he has a crush on Lexi."

Mel gasps. "No!"

"Yes," I say.

"After one day?" She frowns.

"Yes, after one day," I say.

"So, wait." Mel's confused. As she should be. I mean, I was there and I don't even really know how this all happened. "How did you pull off making her think the two of you were a couple?"

"I have to find him," I say, ignoring her. Eventually I am going to have to tell Mel that she supposedly has a crush on Jared, but I can't right now. If she's going to get mad at me, I need to have a clear head to deal with it. Besides, I read this thing somewhere about how if you want to be an effective person, you have to do the thing that's the most important first thing in the morning.

And right now, the most important thing is finding Jared and Lexi and keeping them away from each other. Far, far away. In another state would be okay, even.

"Where is he?" she asks. She squints at herself in the mirror that's stuck to the inside of her locker door and smoothes her hair.

"I have no idea," I say. "But I have to find him." Suddenly I feel sick. Every moment Jared is out of my sight is a moment he could be with Lexi. And every moment he's with Lexi is a moment he could be screwing things up. Ohmigod. What if Jared decides to take things into his own hands and tell Lexi he likes her? Or what if he starts flirting with her? Or what if Lexi decides she should let Jared know she's in on the secret?

"Come on," I say to Mel. "We have to find him." I grab her arm and start pulling her down the hall.

"Devon, calm down," Mel says. "And don't pull my arm like that—it's going to pop out of my socket." She follows me dutifully down the hall, stepping on my heels at one point, but I don't even really notice because I'm so focused on the task at hand.

And then I see him. He's putting his stuff in his locker. Of course he's at his locker. Where else would he be? It's before first period. Everyone is at their lockers!

Why did I not think of that before? I must learn to think logically about this situation and not let myself get out of control with craziness. Otherwise it could cloud my judgment and I could end up missing obvious things, like the fact that Jared would be at his locker before first period.

"Oh, good, there he is," Mel says. She points.

"Shh!" I say, pushing her hand down. "Not so loud!"

"Why?" she asks. "What's the big deal?"

"I dunno," I say. "I can't just be pointing at him!"

"Why not?" Mel frowns. "Go talk to him. Didn't you guys hang out all last night?"

"Yes," I admit. It's one thing to talk to Jared when we're out in a group, when Lexi's around and he thinks I'm hanging out with her. It's quite another thing to just go up to him and initiate conversation. What if he forgot who I am?

"So, go on," Mel says. "At least say hi to him. We have to go that way to get to homeroom, anyway."

"That's okay," I say, watching as Luke comes walking down the hall from the other way. He stops at Jared's locker and they start talking. I'm too far away to hear what they're saying, but I'm sure it's something very important. Something that shouldn't be interrupted.

"Really, all I wanted to do was make sure he wasn't around Lexi. And now that I've done that, I'm fine." I'm lying. Again. I'm not fine. My heart is beating erratically. Jared looks so hot. He's wearing a blue sweater and khaki pants, and his hair is all shiny, like he just got it cut. Which is impossible, I know, since I just saw him last night, and I'm sure he hasn't had time to get his hair cut since then.

"Come on," I whisper at Mel, pulling her down the hallway. "We gotta go."

"Devi!" someone yells from behind me. It sounds like Luke. I ignore it.

"Uh, someone's calling you," Mel says.

"I know," I say. "Just keep going." But then I feel a hand on my back.

"Devi?" Luke says. "Hey."

"Oh, hi," I say, making it out like I didn't hear him. "How are you?"

"I'm good," he says. "Fine." He looks from me to Melissa. "Hi, Melissa," he says.

"Hi," Mel says shyly. How cute! He knows who Mel is.

"Yo," Jared says, coming up behind Luke in the hall. "What's goin' on?"

"Nothing," I say. It comes out as kind of a squeak,

since suddenly my mouth is very, very dry.

Must. Not. Freak. Out.

"Jared and I were just talking about DDR," Luke says, smiling. "He was saying that he and Lexi could beat you and me, but I was telling him that was impossible since you and I are obviously the best at DDR, and therefore we would make an unstoppable team."

What? Why is Jared referring to himself and Lexi as a team? I need to do damage control. Think, Devon, think. Maybe I should make up something really horrible about Lexi. Maybe that she used to be a stalker, and now she's not allowed to date until her probation is up.

"Yeah, Lexi actually doesn't really like DDR," I say. "After last night she said she never really wants to play it again." In actuality, Lexi loves DDR. Over the summer, we'd play at least once a day at the arcade near my grandma's house. We'd take the money Lexi's mom gave her for lunch and change it into quarters, and if we got on a roll, we could make it last for hours. Lexi's mom didn't approve of DDR (she thought it was too boyish), and since the arcade was in the mall, sometimes we'd have to hide behind the pinball machine if we thought we saw one of Mrs. Cortland's friends. It was kind of fun, almost like being undercover agents or something.

"She seemed like she was having fun." Jared frowns.

"Yeah, well, she's a really good actress," I say. This is bad. Horrible, even.

"She used to be in drama at her old school," Mel offers helpfully.

"Yes," I agree. "The drama club. She did plays and all that." Mel and I are nodding our butts off, as if that will make it true.

"Um, okay," Jared says, looking confused. "Did you have a chance to talk to her?"

"Talk to who?" I ask, playing dumb. La, la, la.

"To Lexi," Jared says, sighing. "About what we talked about last night."

Before I can think of something witty and fun that will distract Jared from Lexi, she comes walking down the hall. Talk about horrible timing. Lexi, Mel, Jared, me, and Luke all in the same place. Great.

"Hey, guys!" Lexi trills. She's wearing a short jean skirt over black leggings and a black-and-white striped top. Her hair is straight, shiny, and parted in the middle.

"Hey, there," Jared says, practically drooling.

"Well!" I say. "Time to get to homeroom."

"But the bell hasn't even rung yet," Luke says.

"Yeah, Devi, don't be a dork," Lexi says. She smiles, showing off her braces.

"Yeah, Devi," Mel agrees, nodding. "Don't be a dork." I make a mental note to kill her later.

"We were just talking about DDR," Jared says. "I was saying that you and I could beat Luke and Devi any day of the week."

"Oooh, I don't know," Lexi says. "Devi was pretty good. We used to play all the time over the summer. I made her do it because I just love to—"

"Actually," I say, cutting her off, "I, uh, needed to talk to Jared about the, um, English assignment." I shoot Lexi a look, to convey to her that she should take Luke and Mel away from me and my boyfriend. Then, in the very next moment, I try to give Jared a look that will say, "I need to talk to you about Lexi, that's why I'm making everyone leave" and to Lexi will look like I'm saying, "Jared, I love you and I want to be alone with you, so let's get rid of all these other people."

"Ohhh," Lexi says, getting it. She smiles, and looks at Mel like she's some kind of child who needs to be babysat. "Melissa, right? Can you show me where my homeroom is? I still don't know my way around this place that well." She grabs Mel and leads her away before Mel can answer.

The bell really does ring then. "See you guys later," Luke says, and takes off down the hall.

Oh, thank God. Dodged a huge bullet there. I'm so busy congratulating myself for being so obviously brilliant that I almost forget that I'm supposed to be talking to Jared about a fake conversation I had with Lexi.

"So," he says, looking at me expectantly. Crap. Okay. Deep breath. I try to think logically about the situation, and not get caught up in panic and emotions, but it's hard when he's looking at me like that. His eyes are so blue. I realize how close he is to me, and I remember the way it felt last night when he hugged me after playing DDR. I feel my face start to get hot, and I will myself to focus on the situation.

"So," I say.

"Did you talk to her?" He has a hopeful look on his face. How is this possible? That he likes Lexi? He doesn't even know her! He's hardly talked to her, even. I don't think they're in any of the same classes. Which means Lexi came here yesterday, ate lunch with Jared and the A-list, and not only got herself invited out with them, but also got him to like her. This is so unfair. Not only have I known him longer (if you count sitting near him in English as knowing him), but during all of our exchanges, I've been extremely witty. In fact, one time in English

I brought up this amazing point about theme in *Romeo and Juliet*. And last year, in sixth grade, our teacher read my essay on Christopher Columbus out loud to the whole class. How is Jared not impressed by this?

"Yes," I say slowly. "I did talk to her." Not sure this is the right answer, but I have to say something.

"What did she say?" He's looking at me eagerly. Oh, Jared, why, why, why? Lexi's cute, but so am I! I'm losing it. I'm making up weird love poems in my head. Roses are red, violets are blue, Lexi is cute, but I am too!

"She said, uh, she said . . ." I look around desperately, but there's really only one answer. "She said she's not interested in you like that." Jared looks shocked. Understandably so. I'm sure he's never heard that before. That a girl isn't interested in him like that. Which makes me wonder why he didn't just ask Lexi out himself. Not that I'm complaining. That would have been completely disastrous.

"She doesn't like me?"

"No," I say forcefully, making sure I can drive the point home. The sound of my voice surprises me. Not only am I using my Devi voice, I'm using it to boss Jared around.

"But—" Jared starts. The warning bell rings, signaling

that we only have one minute to get to homeroom. Crap. I'm on the other side of the building. The logistics of all these interventions and stalkings is going to be a nightmare.

"Well," I say. "I should get to homeroom."

"Yeah," he says, still looking confused. "See ya."

Once I'm out of his sight, I kick up my pace a notch so that I'm just short of running. I slide into my seat right before the bell rings. No sweat.

"It's more about what you *think* it means," I say, looking at Mel over the table. We're in the library during study hall, working on our English assignment.

"But that's the problem," Mel says, squinting down at the poem in front of her. "I don't know *what* it means."

"You don't have to," I say. "There's no right or wrong answer." Mel frowns. "That's the point of the exercise. To see how many different interpretations everyone comes up with, and then kind of show that poetry is really what you get out of it, regardless of what the writer intended."

"Oh," she says. "So all I have to do is write what I think it means, and it doesn't matter if it's right or not?"

"Yup."

"Thanks, Devon." She starts writing happily in her English notebook for a second, and then stops. Her eyebrows knit together in concentration. "So, wait, what does it mean?"

"I just told you," I say. "It means whatever you think it means."

"I know teachers always *say* they want you to just interpret it, but what if Mr. Benchley makes us read it out loud in front of the class?"

"I think he's going to," I say. "So that we can hear all the other interpretations."

"Exactly," Mel says, nodding. "So I don't want to write anything that's too crazy, because what if the poem is about sharks or something and I write that it's about the European countryside?"

"I'd go with the European countryside if you had to choose," I say. "I don't think people write too many poems about sharks."

"I think it's about love," Mel says, looking nervous.

"That's what I wrote too," I say. "That it's about love."

"You did?" Mel asks. She picks up her pen again. "And you feel okay about reading that out loud?"

"Why wouldn't I?" Hmm, except for the fact that

Jared is in my class, and my interpretation is about unrequited love. Maybe he'll think I'm writing about him and Lexi. Sigh.

"Remember what happened last year? When the whole sixth grade had to write a poem for Celebrating Literature Week? And Brianna Hazelton wrote that poem about love, and everyone laughed at her?"

I giggle, thinking about Brianna's poem. "Mel, Brianna used the words 'quivering loins' and 'bated breath.' Just stay away from anything cheesy and you'll be fine."

Mel giggles. "So what's the deal with you babysitting so much lately?" she asks. She consults the poem again, reads over a line, and then starts writing.

"What do you mean?" I ask.

"You've just been babysitting Katie a lot lately."

"Oh," I say, not sure how to respond. I *have* been babysitting Katie a lot lately, mostly because my parents have been at therapy, or making sure to go out on "dates." But since Mel has no idea what went on with my parents this summer, I can't exactly tell her that. "Yeah, it has to do with my mom's work. She's going out a lot with her clients, and she takes my dad with her."

"That's cool," Mel says, accepting this. "Sucks that you have to watch Katie, though."

"I don't really mind," I say, which is true.

"I wish my parents would go out more often," she says. "All they do is sit around the house and do puzzles." Mel's parents are the most normal parents you'll ever meet. They're like a couple you'd see on TV. They do puzzles, and go for long walks with their dogs, and make organic food in their blender. A lot of times on weekends, they get super excited about watching documentaries that they order from Netflix. Which is one of the reasons it was easier to tell Lexi about the stuff with my parents. Lexi's dad was never really around, and her mom is kind of crazy.

"Yeah," I say. I pull our BFF notebook out of my bag, and while Mel finishes her English, I start writing her a note. I think maybe writing in the notebook will help me feel better about the fact that I lied to Lexi about Mel liking Jared. But when the bell rings, signaling the end of study hall, I don't feel any better at all.

Lunch. Things are about to take a turn for the worst. I'm standing at the front of the cafeteria with Melissa, wondering what I should do. The problem is that Lexi is nowhere to be found. She's not sitting with the A-list and she's not in the lunch line. I can't just go marching up to Jared's table without her.

"What are we gonna do?" Mel asks.

"I dunno," I say. "Just stand here for a while, probably."

"That's ridiculous," Mel says. "We can't just stand here forever."

"Not forever," I say, "Just until, you know, I figure out what to do."

"So yeah, forever."

I move out of the way as Matt O'Connor goes flying by me with a full tray of food. If we stand here much longer, we're going to get run over. Ketchup and food stains all over me is definitely not going to be a good look, especially when I'm trying to pretend I'm Devi.

"Hey!" someone says behind me. I turn around to see Luke standing there. "What's going on?"

"Oh, nothing," I say, trying to look nonchalant. "Mel and I were just waiting for Lexi." Which isn't a lie. We *were* kind of waiting for Lexi.

"Come sit with us," Luke says. "She'll probably be here soon."

I shrug. "Okay," I say. "Cool." Mel and I follow Luke to his table. I hope we look casual, like we're used to this. I practice my Devi walk. Devi, up until this point, hasn't had a walk, but I think it's time she gets one. I practice relaxing my legs while I walk, and almost trip over the back of Luke's shoes.

"Oh," Kim says when she sees Mel and I intend to sit down at her table. "Who invited you guys to sit here?"

"Um, Luke did," I mumble.

"Luke?" she repeats. "*Luke* asked you to sit here?" She seems mad.

"Um, yeah." So much for my Devi voice.

"Well, whatev," she says, rolling her eyes. Hmm. Maybe Kim's just having a bad day. She seemed fine last night at the arcade. I decide to make an effort to be nice.

"So!" I say brightly, sliding into the chair next to her. "How's your day going, Kim?"

She looks at me like I'm a leper. "It's going fine," she says. "Except that I got a D on my French paper." She rolls her eyes. "Which is insane, because, hello, I've actually been to France."

"That sucks," I say. I rip open my carton of chocolate milk and take a sip. "But if you're having trouble in French, I can help you. I actually—"

I realize then that Kim is ignoring me. She's turned to Kayleigh Trusco, who is sitting on the other side of her and is blathering away about some movie she saw last weekend. Well. Okay then.

"This is awkward," Mel whispers. She's sitting across from me.

"How so?" I say.

"No one is talking to us." She's right. No one *is* talking to us. Luke is all the way at the other end of the table, apparently forgetting that he invited us to sit here. Not that I expect him to babysit us, but still. It would have been nice if he hadn't just left us to fend for ourselves. Jared's down at the other end of the table as well, which may be problematic if Lexi shows up. How am I going to explain the fact that I'm not sitting near him? Although I suppose I should be grateful I'm even at this table at all. That in itself is a small miracle.

"They just don't know us, that's all," I tell Mel. "They're usually really nice." Mel raises her eyebrows.

"Devi!" Lexi comes rushing up behind me and throws her arms around my back. "I'm so sorry I'm late." She sits down on the other side of the table next to Mel. "I had to go to guidance again." She rolls her eyes and pulls the top off of her yogurt. "Mr. Boone thinks I need help with 'the challenges of acclimating to a new school.' Isn't that crazy?" She throws her head back and laughs. The overhead lights bounce off her braces.

"That's nuts," I say. Lexi obviously needs no help acclimating to a new school. She's been here one day, is sitting at the popular kids' lunch table, and has the hottest guy in school crushing on her. If Mr. Boone is interested in helping kids, he should talk to his existing students and help *them* get acclimated to school. Lexi could teach him how to do it.

"I know," Lexi says, sighing. She reaches over and takes a sip of my milk. Right out of my straw and everything. "I told him I don't need help acclimating, that I already have friends here, and that nothing is wrong." She sighs again. "And then I was like, hello! If you're worried about me making friends, you should stop calling me out of lunch, because obviously I'm going to need social interaction."

"Good point," I say.

"So what'd I miss?" She scans the table, and notices Jared at the other end. "Oh!" she exclaims. "Why aren't you—" Then she notices Melissa. "Oh, hi," she says politely. She gives me a knowing look.

This is bad. This is very, very bad. What if Mel says something about me and Jared being together?

And then Lexi will be all, "But I thought you liked him, Mel, so what's the deal?"

"Hi," Mel says. I relax slightly. Mel wouldn't say anything about the Jared thing. She's way smarter than that. She wouldn't—

"So, how was the mall last night?" Mel asks.

Lexi frowns. My stomach drops.

"Um, Mel?" I say, bolting up out of my chair. "Could I talk to you for a second?"

"Sure." She looks startled, but follows me into the girls' bathroom that's attached to the cafeteria.

"So I did something bad," I say once we're standing in front of the sinks. Please don't be mad, please don't be mad, please don't be mad. I chant this over and over in my head, figuring if I say it enough times, it might come true.

"Besides creating a whole secret life for yourself?" she asks, rolling her eyes.

"Yes, actually," I say. "Besides that." The sound of a toilet flushing comes out of one of the stalls, and a random eighth grader comes out and starts washing her hands. I pull Mel over to the side.

"Okay," Mel says slowly. "Are you going to tell me?"

"So yesterday, when I was talking to Lexi about how Jared and I were together, I had to give her a reason not to tell anyone." Please don't be mad, please don't be mad, please don't be mad.

"And?" Mel says, her eyes narrowing suspiciously.

"Well, I kind of accidentally told her that the reason she couldn't tell anyone about it is because Jared and I are dating in secret."

"Dating in secret?" Mel's expression turns from suspicion to confusion. Her blue eyes crinkle, and I feel horrible.

"Yeah," I say slowly. "And the reason I told her we were dating in secret is because I said you have a secret crush on him." I hold my breath and wait for the explosion.

"WHAT?!" Mel shrieks. "Devon! Why would you do something like that?"

"Because," I say, "I don't know, I don't know, I just panicked and I got nervous and I didn't know what to do. It just kind of popped out." I bite my lip. This is definitely not worth it. If Mel is upset with me to the point where she's going to go ballistic and get really mad, I need to put an end to this whole thing right now.

"But I don't like Jared not even one little bit!" Mel says. She throws her hands up in exasperation. I notice she's wearing new, pink nail polish.

"I like your nail polish," I say, taking her hand in mind. "Very glam."

"Don't try to change the subject," she says. She folds her arms across her chest. "I can't believe you did that, Devon! Of all the people! Jared Bentley! You know how I feel about him. With his gelled hair and his gym clothes and . . ." she trails off, like Jared is so horrible, she can't even finish the sentence. I'm willing to overlook the fact that she's saying these things about my future husband because she is obviously distressed.

"You're right," I say. "I shouldn't have done that. And I'm going to fix it. I'm going to go out there right now and tell Lexi and everyone the truth." Well, maybe not everyone. There has to be a way I can maybe sort of pull Lexi over to the side and whisper it to her. And then beg her not to tell anyone, ever in her life. I rack my brain for some kind of secret I have, something I can use to blackmail Lexi with. But there's nothing. She's perfect. Which is why Jared likes her. "Seriously, Mel, it's not worth it. Even if I get blacklisted and my life is ruined, it's not fair to you. I'm going to tell the truth." I start walking out of the bathroom, but Mel grabs my arm

"No, wait," she says, sighing. She bites her lip and

considers the situation. "Lexi's the only one who thinks I like him?"

"Yes," I say. "She's the only one."

"Fine," Mel says. "I don't care, whatever."

"Thank you, thank you, thank you," I say, hugging her. I feel like jumping up and down.

"But, Devon," she says, pulling away and looking at me seriously. "You are going to have to stop this."

"I know," I say. "It's just until I can stage a fake breakup, I promise." Or until I can get Jared to fall in love with me. I make a cross over my heart to show Mel how serious I am.

When Mel and I get back to the lunch table, somehow the seating arrangements have changed, and Jared is now sitting across from Lexi. What? Why?

"It's a totally awesome movie," Jared's saying. "I have it on DVD." He looks at her expectantly, waiting for her to invite herself over to watch it. Or at least hint that she wants to. Thankfully, Lexi thinks Jared is a taken man, so she doesn't get the hint. What is Jared doing, anyway? Why would he be flirting with Lexi when I just told him SHE DOESN'T LIKE HIM LIKE THAT?

Geez. "Uh, Jared?" I say, smiling at him sweetly. "Can I talk to you for a second?"

"Sure," he says. He stands up and follows me to the side of the cafeteria. Lexi gives me a knowing look. Kim glares at me (what's up with that?), and Mel just shakes her head.

"So, listen," I say to Jared once we're out of earshot. "I thought I told you Lexi doesn't like you." Suddenly I'm very aware of the fact that Jared and I are having a private conversation. I also realize that I initiated this conversation, which is something I never would have done two days ago. Not only am I lying, but I'm acting like a completely different person. This thought worries me for some reason, so I push it out of my head and concentrate on making sure I use my Devi voice.

"Yeah, I know," he says. "But I figured maybe if I talked to her, got to know her, she might change her mind."

"No," I say simply. "She won't."

"Why not?" he asks, frowning. Good question.

"Because Lexi is very determined," I say. "She's very, uh, *strong-willed*."

"Strong-willed?" He looks skeptical. What is his problem? Has he never run into a strong-willed woman before?

"Yes," I say. "She doesn't like guys falling all over her, because that's what she's used to." Jared turns to look at Lexi, and at that moment, unknowingly and brilliantly, Matt O'Connor sits down in the seat Jared was just sitting in and starts talking to Lexi. "See?" I say triumphantly. "Guys are falling all over her. Poor Matt." I shake my head. "Lexi's going to crush his heart to bits."

"I see what you mean," Jared says. He does?

"Uh, you do?"

"Yes," Jared says, nodding. "What you're saying is to play hard to get."

"Yes," I say, nodding emphatically. "Yes. Hard to get. Very hard to get. The harder to get, the better."

"Thanks, Devi," Jared says, grinning. "You're awesome." But when he turns around and walks back to the table, I don't feel that awesome. All I feel is horrible.

"We're going to be partnering up for our first major project of the year," Mrs. Vasquez, my social studies teacher, announces later that afternoon. I glance around the room, wondering who I can ask to be my partner. "And I'll be choosing the partners for you." She looks down at us from the front of the room. Great. I hate when teachers pick our partners. I always end up with someone who expects me to do all the work. Or, even worse, someone who wants to do all the work himself, and makes it into this horrible project that I've had no say over.

Mrs. Vasquez moves down the rows, pointing at people and assigning them partners. She seems to be doing it totally randomly. I hold my breath, waiting to see who my partner is. "Devon Delaney and"—she glances down at the seating chart in her hand—"Luke Nichols." We smile at each other nervously.

"So," Luke says, once we've pushed our desks together. "Do you have any idea what you want to do the project on?" Richard Nixon? Bill Clinton? Any of the lying presidents should do the trick.

"Nope," I say. "You?" That's the other problem with school projects. The teachers either assign you some totally ridiculous topic that you have no interest in, or they leave it up to you, and you can never decide on something really cool, so you end up just picking something that inevitably turns out to be really lame. I wonder if we could get away with just doing a diorama. Those are always easy. And we always have plenty of shoe boxes hanging around the house since Katie needs lots of different footwear for all her different Olympic sports.

"I was thinking we could do something on the signing of the Declaration of Independence," Luke says. "We could get everyone to help us do a video, like a reenactment." So much for no one having any cool ideas. How fun!

"That's awesome," I say. "It'll be totally different from anything anyone else is doing."

"We'll just have to make sure we don't look like slackers," Luke says.

"What do you mean?"

"It's just that sometimes teachers figure if you're doing a video or something fun, you're not doing a good job. So we'll have to make sure it's extra good."

"Okay," I say. I pull out a piece of paper in an effort to show Luke that I'm serious about the project. "Should we make a list of things we need?" I grab a pink sparkly pen from my bag.

"Well, the video camera, obviously," Luke says.

"Video cam," I write. "Hmm, I don't have one of those. Do you?"

"No," he says. "But Jared's dad does. I'll ask him if we can use it, and maybe we can all get together this weekend and try to think of some ideas."

My mood brightens a little as I think of being able to hang out with Jared this weekend. "Cool," I say.

"Let me get your phone number," Luke says. "And your screen name, in case we need to make plans."

"Um, okay," I say. I write my number and screen

name down on his notebook. It's the first time a boy has asked for my number, and even though it's only for a school project, a small thrill runs through my body. I concentrate on making my handwriting look cute. I debate whether to write Devi or Devon, and then decide on Devon, since if he calls my house and asks for Devi, my parents are going to wonder why.

"Thanks," he says. He leans in close to me. "They're doing a diorama," he whispers, motioning to Randy Weisman and Laina Peterson, who are sitting next to us. "How lame." He smiles. Right.

"Don't get mad," Lexi says to me at the end of the day as we walk out of school and toward the buses. "But your boyfriend was totally mean to me today!" She puffs out her lip and puts a pouty look on her face.

"Whaddya mean?" I ask, and glance around quickly, just in case anyone's overheard her and is going to burst out with, "What boyfriend? Devon doesn't have a boyfriend." But then I relax slightly when I realize that Lexi thinks Jared is my *secret* boyfriend, so if anyone were to say "What boyfriend? Devon doesn't have a boyfriend," it would actually be okay since no one but Lexi is supposed to know.

"I was walking out of math, and I passed him in the hall, and I said, 'Hey, Jared, what's up? Should be a fun weekend,' and he completely ignored me!" She sighs and runs her hands through her hair.

"Oh," I say. "Maybe he didn't hear you?"

"Oh, he heard me all right," she says. She swings her pink backpack over her shoulder and quickens her pace. The shoes she's wearing make slapping noises against the concrete.

"He was probably in a bad mood," I say, not sure if I'm supposed to be thankful that Jared is taking my advice and blowing Lexi off, or upset because what's the use of having a secret boyfriend if everyone thinks he's a jerk?

"Maybe," Lexi says. She looks thoughtful. "Or maybe he's *pretending* to be mean to your friends in an effort to throw everyone off track."

"Probably," I say nonchalantly. "He's very good at respecting our secret."

"Yeah, well, you may want to talk to him about that again," Lexi says. "Because I saw Mel rolling her eyes at you when you got up to talk to him in the caf. It was totally obvious you two were having some sort of secret conference!" She winks at me. "Is she coming this weekend?"

"Is who coming this weekend?" I ask. It's starting to become hard to keep all my lies straight, and Lexi talks so fast that it's hard for me to focus on her words.

"Mel," Lexi says. "Ohmigod, we have to go shopping!"

"Wait, what?" I say. Head. Spinning. It feels like I have my own personal merry-go-round in my brain.

"We have to go shopping," Lexi says. "And get something for this weekend. I know it's just a school project and all, but it's still going to be fun. And everyone here dresses a little bit different than they did in my old school." She blows her bangs out of her face.

"This weekend," I say. "What's going on this weekend?"

"Hello!" she says. "The video? At Jared's house? God, Devi, it's *your* project!"

"Oh," I say. "I just didn't know you knew about it, that's all." Geez. What is up with this girl? She is PLUGGED IN.

"Of course I know about it," she says. "Kim invited me last period." Oh, good. So now not only is Lexi coming, but Kim is coming too. Great. For some reason, I have a feeling things will be more complicated with Kim around. I can fool Lexi around the boys, but with Kim, it could be trickier.

"So do you want to?" Lexi asks. We're at her bus now, and we stop walking. Her shoes stop clacking. "Go shopping for something to wear?"

"Sure," I say. I should get some new, glam clothes. Something to wear to Jared's, and then, I don't know, like a whole other wardrobe, perhaps? I wonder how I'm going to get my mom to give me money for the clothes.

"Call ya later, Devi," Lexi says, and then hops onto her bus.

chapter five

"Absolutely not," my mom says later that night when I ask my parents if I can have money for new clothes. "You got a lot of new clothes this summer."

"But I can't wear my summer clothes now," I say. Duh. "And I don't really have any nice school clothes." I'm trying to play the "I have nothing to wear to school" angle, figuring "new school clothes" sounds way better than "new clothes to convince people I'm popular."

"What exactly do you need, Devon?" my dad asks from the kitchen table, where he's reading the paper.

Katie's sitting next to him, drawing a picture of a soccer player.

"David!" my mom says. She starts pulling plates down from the cabinets, setting the table for dinner. "She got enough clothes over the summer."

"I know," my dad says. "But she can't wear those now." My mom frowns, and I start to get worried. If my parents are going to get in a fight over this, it's so not worth it. I can't really remember the last time they had a fight, but I do remember they fought a lot before Katie and I went away for the summer. No way I want to go back to that. "Maybe we can compromise," my dad says, and I relax. It seems like that's a big part of their counseling appointments. The whole compromise thing.

"Yes," I say. "Let's compromise." My dad winks at me over his paper, and I wink back.

"What kind of compromise?" my mom asks. She sets a plate down on the table.

"Well," my dad says, folding his paper and standing up. "Maybe Devon could be allowed to get a few new things, as long as she doesn't spend too much money. There's no reason she needs to spend as much money as she did this summer, but she should have the things she needs." He starts collecting silverware from the silverware drawer. My dad is really trying to show my mom that he takes her new job seriously, even though she's working from home. He's constantly helping around the house.

"Well," my mom says, looking thoughtful.

"Mo-om," I say. "Come onnn. I watched Katie all last night." I'm not above whining.

"Yes," my mom says, "and you got to go out anyway."

"So?" I say. "It's not like we were doing anything bad. We went to the mall."

"We played DDR," Katie says from her spot at the kitchen table.

"What is DDR?" my mom asks, her blue eyes narrowing suspiciously. Every day at four o'clock, my mom takes a break from her work and settles into the living room couch with a cup of tea to watch *Oprah* and *Dr. Phil*. Because of this, she knows about all the scary teen trends that are going on throughout middle-class America and is therefore nervous whenever she hears a term that she doesn't know the definition of.

"It's nothing," I say, resisting the urge to roll my eyes. "It's just this game they have at the arcade."

"Yes." Katie nods in agreement. "It's a dance game."

"Well, I've never heard of it," my mom says, looking at me closely. Probably for signs that it's not really a dance game but something else, something that involves internet predators or street gangs.

"What does 'DDR' stand for?" my dad asks.

"Dance Dance Revolution," I tell him.

"How do you play?" he asks, looking intrigued. My dad loves arcades and video games. Sometimes on Sundays we drive out to this place in Hartford called Blinky's. It's a huge arcade with tons of games. We spend all afternoon there, just hanging out and playing, and then we go to lunch and order two entrées each, and bring home whatever's left over. I wonder if my dad would be good at DDR.

"I told you," Katie says. "It's for dancing. Like this." She gets up off her chair and starts hitting her feet against the floor.

"Yes, great, Katie, that's how you do it," I say, trying to keep my patience. I remind myself Katie is only five years old, and someday may become a famous Olympian and I might need to borrow money from her.

"Don't be mean to me, Devon," Katie says. "Thank you very much."

"I wasn't being mean to you," I say. "But I'm trying to talk to Mom and Dad about something, and you keep interrupting. You interrupt a lot."

"I do not," Katie says. She puts her hands on her

hips. "I did not interrupt last night when you were playing the dancing game with your boyfriend."

"Boyfriend?" my mom gasps. "What is she talking about?"

"I have no idea," I say, shrugging. I put an innocent look on my face. "I don't have a boyfriend." This is not a lie. Well, depending on who you ask, anyway. My mom and dad exchange a look, one of those "Who's going to talk to her about this?" looks.

The phone rings, saving me, but Katie gets to it first. "Hello, Delaney household, this is Katie speaking, how may I help you today?" I don't understand why my mom lets her answer the phone like that. You'd think Oprah would have had a show about not letting your five-year-old give her name out to any random stranger who happens to call your house.

"It's for you," Katie says to me, thrusting the phone in my face.

It's Mel.

"Hey," she says. "Is everything all right? I waited for you after school today." Whoops. I completely forgot Mel and I were supposed to walk to our buses together.

"I'm so sorry," I say. "I ran into Lexi and then things just got completely out of control."

"Oh," she says. Silence.

"I'm really sorry," I say again.

"It's okay," she says, not sounding like it is. "I was just worried."

The call waiting beeps in my ear. "Can you hang on a second?" I ask Mel.

"Sure," Mel says, sounding slightly exasperated, like my dad does when Katie asks him to put the gold medal around her neck. (Katie has a gold medal that's made out of tinfoil and cardboard. Which makes it look silver even though it's supposed to be the gold medal. Katie got around this little detail by writing "GOLD MEDAL" on it in black Sharpie, in case there's any confusion.)

"Hello," I say. "Delaney residence, this is Devon speaking, how many I help you?" I stick my tongue out at Katie to show her how ridiculous I think her phone greeting is.

"Hey, Devi," a male voice says in my ear. "It's Luke."

"Oh," I say, trying to think of what I could say to make up for the fact that I just answered the phone in the same way my slightly delusional five-year-old sister does. "What's up?"

"Not much," he says easily. "Listen, I just wanted

to let you know that I talked to Jared, and he's fine with us using his camera and his house this weekend. Can you do it Saturday at around two?"

"Oh, definitely," I say. I make a mental note to ask my mom if it's okay. Which it will have to be, since I've already said yes, and everyone knows it's quite rude to cancel plans.

"Who's that?" Katie asks. She starts pulling on my shirt. "Who's that on the phone?"

I ignore her and move to the other side of the refrigerator, out of her sight. I consider switching to the cordless phone but realize that to do so, I will have to leave this phone while I go get the cordless phone, and whoever hangs it up for me (i.e., Katie or one of my parents) might realize I'm on the phone with a boy and/or say something potentially embarrassing.

"Great," Luke says. "So we should probably get together at some point before that, to go over the script and figure out who's going to play what parts. I'm pretty sure everyone wants to do it—Jared, Kim, Lexi, Matt O'Connor . . ."

"Good idea," I say.

"Mo-oomm," Katie says. "Devon's being mean to me."

"Devon, I'd like you to get off the phone now," my

mom says. "We were in the middle of a discussion." I ignore them both.

"Do you have to go?" Luke asks. He sounds concerned.

"Oh," I say. "No, why?" The last thing I want is Luke thinking I'm not allowed to use the phone like a normal person. Not to mention the way I answered it.

"I thought I heard your mom say you had to get off the phone."

"Oh, no," I say, "She was talking to my sister." I cover the mouthpiece with my hand. "Mom," I whisper. "I'll be off in a second, I'm talking about schoolwork." Why is it when I'm lying, people believe me, and when I'm telling the truth, they don't? Is it possible I've wrecked my karma so badly that now no one will believe me when I tell the truth? Am I The Girl Who Cried Boyfriend?

"So when do you want to do it?" Luke asks. "It's probably better to do it outside of school."

"Do you want to come over here?" I ask. "Maybe tomorrow afternoon or something? That way, we could write the script, and we could kind of go over it with everybody on Thursday and Friday at lunch." I say the last part nonchalantly, like it's a given that I'll be sitting at the A-list lunch table.

"Cool," he says. "So we'll talk more about this tomorrow?" His voice sounds deeper on the phone than it does in person. I wonder if it's like that with all boys. I've never really talked to a boy on the phone before. Well, except my dad when he calls from work. But I've never really noticed a difference in his voice. Oh, and one time Mel and I called Brent Madison's house last year to see if he would maybe go to the sixth-grade dance with Mel. But we chickened out and hung up on him pretty much as soon as he answered, so I never really got a chance to see if his voice sounded different or not.

"Yeah," I say. "See ya tomorrow, Luke." I turn around to hang up the phone and almost slam into my mother, who is standing right behind me. "Whoa," I say. Her shoulder is pressed up against my nose. I take a step back.

"Was that a boy?" she asks. She takes the phone out of my hand and crosses the kitchen to set it back on the receiver. Her ponytail swings back and forth as she walks.

"Yes," I say. No sense in lying to her since I'm going to have to ask permission to have him over. "That was Luke Nichols. We're working together on a social studies project."

"Is that your boyfriend?" my mom asks. Katie's still sitting at the table, working on her picture, but my dad is nowhere to be found. This makes me instantly nervous, since this probably means my mom told him to go upstairs while she talks to me about this whole boyfriend thing. I can tell she's trying to play it casual, get me to admit something by luring me into a false sense of security.

"No, Mom," I say. "Luke's not my boyfriend."

"He's not," Katie agrees. She reaches into an open box of macaroni that's sitting on the table and takes out a piece of ziti. "Her boyfriend's name is Jared, and I would like to make a macaroni necklace, please."

"Not right now, Kates," my mom says. She takes the box of macaroni from Katie and sets it by the stove. "Maybe after dinner."

"Okay," Katie says, shrugging, which I find slightly disappointing. I was half-hoping Katie would start pitching a fit, therefore sparing me any more embarrassing questions from my mom about my love life.

"So your boyfriend's name is Jared," my mom says, studying me. She wanders over to the stove and pulls a pan down from the cabinet overhead, then heads to the sink and starts filling it with water.

"No," I say. "Jared is not my boyfriend." Again, depending on who you ask.

"But he went to the mall with you," my mom says slowly. She sets the pot on the stove and turns on the burner.

"Yup," Katie says. "He went to the mall." Since when did my sister become Page Six? She pulls her gold medal out of the pocket of her shorts and hands it to me. "Devon," she instructs, "crown me the winner."

"Yes, he went to the mall with me," I tell my mom. I slip the piece of cardboard around Katie's neck. "Katherine Grace Delaney, I now pronounce you winner of the gold medal in soccer for the third year in row. The United States thanks you for being such a good athlete and bestowing this honor upon our nation." Katie puts her hand over her heart and starts humming the national anthem softly to herself. "Anyway," I say, turning back to my mom. "Luke is going to come over tomorrow so we can work on our project, okay?"

"I guess it's okay," my mom says. She bites her lip. "Devon, if you're interested in boys, that's okay. It's normal at your age."

"Mom," I say, "I don't have a boyfriend."

"Okay," she says, sounding doubtful. I wonder what my mom would think if she knew what was really going on, all the lying and the manipulating. I don't think she'd be too pleased. I take a deep breath and try to push those thoughts to the back of my mind. It's going to be fine. In fact, things are going great. I just have to give it a few days, keep Jared away from Lexi, stage a fake breakup, and everything will go back to the way it was. I have everything under control.

The phone rings again, and Katie hops down from the kitchen chair that she's using as a podium and grabs it. "Delaney household, this is Katie speaking, how may I help you please?" She pauses and then holds the phone out to me. "It's for you Devon. It's Melissa. You left her on the other line. Not very nice." She hands me the phone and hops away happily. Everything under control. Right.

"This afternoon is going to be so fun, Devi!" Lexi squeals the next morning before homeroom. I'm standing in front of my locker, trying to figure out what books I need for the morning. My eyes feel scratchy and tired, like someone rubbed them with sandpaper. I had a hard time sleeping last night. Probably because of all the stress. Plus I got to bed late. I was up trying to find something to wear to school. I went through all my clothes at least a thousand times, but I couldn't find anything that seemed cool enough. I couldn't even find a way to make any of my summer clothes warmer. They should really teach us more about sewing our own clothes in home and careers. Right now all we learn how to do is hem and sew on buttons. Which is useless, because I'm trying to make my clothes warmer, not shorter.

"Yes, Lexi," I say, my voice purposely low so maybe she'll get the hint that it's good to be quiet. Speaking of voices, my Devi voice still comes and goes. Sometimes I remember to use it, sometimes I don't. I sound like guys do when their voice is changing. Except I'm a girl. So it's not exactly the best sound. No one's said anything yet, but I'm just waiting for one of them to bust out with, "DEVON, WHY DO YOU KEEP SWITCHING YOUR VOICE?" It's like pretending to have an accent or something. "It's going to be fun."

"We have to hit Nordstrom," she says. She grabs my locker door and swings it out, almost hitting me in the face. "Devi, where's your mirror?" She frowns.

"I don't have one," I say.

"You don't have one? Why not?" She runs her hands through her hair and pulls a small mirror out of her purse. "Never mind, we'll get you one today." She runs her tongue over her braces and smiles at her reflection.

"Listen, I have to be home by six," I tell her. I slam my locker door shut. The metal makes a clanging noise that reverberates through the hall.

"That doesn't give us much time," she says, frowning. "Why do you have to be home so early?" She leans in close to me and lowers her voice. "Is everything okay with your parents?"

"Yeah," I say. "Everything's totally fine." In fact, last night my parents stayed up until after midnight, watching DVDs and giggling in the family room. I know this because I was still awake and I could hear them all the way upstairs. It was nice of Lexi to ask, though, and I realize how cool it will be to spend time alone, just the two of us, without having to worry about anyone else being around, saying things that could cause problems. Not only is this whole lie causing problems in my friendship with Mel, but with Lexi also. I swallow around the lump in my throat.

"Cool," Lexi says. "So why do you have to be home?"

"Because Luke is coming over to work on our project," I tell her. I don't tell her my mom is sketched out because she thinks Luke might be my boyfriend.

"Fun," Lexi says, rolling her eyes. "I gotta get to homeroom." She flounces off down the hall, her hair bouncing behind her and her skirt flouncing. Lexi is very flouncy.

"Where were you this morning?" Mel asks me later in study hall. "I waited for you by my locker." Crap. I totally forgot that I was supposed to meet Mel this morning. That's the second time in two days I've forgotten about her.

"I'm so sorry," I tell her. "I got to school late and I was rushing around to make it to homeroom on time." Which isn't actually that much of a lie. I did get to school late. My mom had to drive me because I missed my bus. I'm still struggling to keep my eyes open after my late night.

"That's okay," Mel says. She pulls open her binder and takes out a sheet of paper. "Did you work on the English assignment?"

"No," I say. "I didn't get a chance to start it last night. I was busy planning some of my social studies project." And looking for clothes to wear until really, really late.

"Oh," she says, looking a little disappointed.

"But we can work on it now," I say, pulling out my book. "It probably won't be that hard."

"Cool," she says, pulling out her English anthology. "Did you get a chance to write in the notebook?"

I pull our BFF notebook out of my bag and hand it to her. I finished the note I had started writing to her in study hall last night. It was one of the things I did while staying up super late. I wrote her a really nice note, talking about how much I appreciated everything she's done for me lately. Of course, I kept a lot of it deliberately vague, since, you know, I wouldn't want it falling into the wrong hands.

"Thanks," Mel says. She slips it into her bag just as Brent Madison walks by our table.

"Hey, Melissa," he says, nodding his head at her as he goes by. He's with his friends James Johnson and Brad Button, and they nod at us as well. They're all in their football jerseys, since our school has a game tonight.

"Hey," Mel squeaks back. A stunned look comes over her face.

"Ohmigod, ohmigod, ohmigod!" I shriek once Brent is out of earshot. Melissa has had a crush on

Brent since, like, forever. Last year at the sixth-grade dance she spent the whole time obsessing over whether or not she should ask him to dance. She finally decided to go for it, except by then, Brent was gone. We found out later he had to leave early because he was going on a family vacation the next morning. It's still one of Mel's biggest regrets.

"That's the first time he's ever said hi to me," Mel says, looking shocked.

"That's crazy," I say. "And he gave you the nod, too."

"The nod?" Mel asks.

"Yeah, the head nod that goes with the hi," I say. "And it was the good kind of head nod."

"The good kind?" Mel is starting to look dazed. I hope I'm not overloading her with too much info.

"Yes," I explain. "See, if a guy gives you a nod when he says hi, it depends on which way he moves his head if it's good or not. If he moves it up, it means he's doing it in a flirty way. If he moves it down, it means he's just doing it to be friendly."

"And he moved his head up?" Mel asks, twirling a strand of hair around her finger and looking thoughtful.

"Yes," I say.

"And how do you know that means it's flirty?"

"I read it in *CosmoGIRL!*," I report. In addition to the romance novels, I read a lot of magazines this summer. Lexi and I would walk to the drugstore near her house and buy every magazine we could get our hands on, along with sodas and bags of chips and Swedish Fish. Then we'd hang out on my grandma's porch for hours, reading, talking, and eating our snacks.

"But what if—"

"Hey, Devi," Kim says, sitting down next to me at the long table. Oh. I totally forgot she was in this study hall. Probably because she never speaks to me. "What's going on?" She's wearing long white flared pants and a long-sleeved emerald green shirt that says ROCKSTAR on it in gold lettering. She also has what appears to be purple glitter on her eyes. My mom won't even let me wear makeup, much less purple glitter. I wonder what Kim's mom is like. Probably like Paris Hilton's mom. Very glam.

"Not much," I say, finally remembering to use my Devi voice, even though I'm slightly surprised that she's speaking to me. Not just because she's Kim, but because she was so frosty to me in the caf the other day. Maybe she has multiple personality disorder.

That could be why all the guys want her. Isn't that what they say? That guys want someone who keeps them guessing?

"I'm psyched for tonight," Kim says. She flips her long hair behind her back and blinks at me. Sparkle, sparkle.

"What's tonight?" I ask.

"We're going to the mall," she says. "You, me, and Lexi." She glances at Melissa, who opens up her English book and pretends to be reading. I can tell she's just pretending because her eyes are not moving across the page.

"Oh," I say. "I didn't know you were coming." What is it with these people and making plans? And how does word travel so quickly? Is there some kind of communication chain? And if so, how do I get plugged into it? I'm disappointed that Kim's coming. Not only will it be trickier because of the whole Jared lie situation, but I was looking forward to hanging out with Lexi by myself.

"Yup," she says. "Lexi invited me this morning. I totally need to get my nails done." She puts her hands out and studies her fingers critically. She's wearing a perfect coat of purple sparkly nail polish, which matches her purple sparkly eye glitter. I wonder if she has different colors of glittery polish and shadow to match her different outfits.

"Cool," I say. "It should be really fun."

"Yup," Kim says. "It will be. Just the three of us."

Mel's nose twitches, but she keeps her face in the book and her nonmoving eyes on the page.

chapter six

"Try this one," Lexi says, handing me a bright red lip gloss. It's after school, and I'm in Sephora with her and Kim, trying out different shades of lip gloss. The cool thing about Sephora is that you can try everything in the store, so you never have to worry about stuff looking silly on you.

"Are you sure?" I take the tube from Lexi and smear the gloss on my lips. I peer into the mirror over the display. I look like a clown.

"Um, that would be a no," Kim says, handing me a tissue.

"Thanks," I say, wiping it off and wondering if she

meant that in a mean way. Even so, shopping with Lexi and Kim is FUN. First, we stopped at Bavarian Pretzel and got orange freezies to carry around with us as we shopped. Then we went to Nordstrom, where Lexi bought three pairs of capri pants (which doesn't make a lot of sense since it's fall, but they were on sale and she swore she would regret not buying them when the weather got warm) and Kim bought a pair of jeans.

We hit the arcade and DDR'd for a little while, and then went to Old Navy, where I got two pairs of jeans and three shirts that are wicked cute. The best part is that I still have about seventy dollars left over.

"This one's better for you," Kim says, handing me a pink sparkly color. I put some on and inspect myself in the mirror. She's right. Much better.

"I can't decide between 'Twinkled Pink' eye shadow and 'Ice Storm,'" she says, frowning at the two containers in her hand.

"Better get them both," I instruct, figuring it's what Devi would say.

"Good thinking," Kim says, nodding in agreement. "After all, there's nothing wrong with splurging if you know you're going to be hanging out with someone special."

"Right," I say, not sure what she means by that. Is she talking about this weekend? Does Kim like Jared? I decide not to worry about it. I have my hands full trying to keep Kim from saying anything that would lead Lexi to believe that we've never hung out before. It actually hasn't been that hard, and there was only one close call, when we were in Old Navy and Kim was all, "What size are you?" while she was helping me look for a certain pair of jeans I wanted and Lexi was like, "Don't you know?" like she figured Kim and I go shopping together all the time. And then Kim gave this sort of puzzled look, and I quickly said, "I'm not sure what size I wear here. This store always runs big for some reason," which seemed to satisfy Lexi. I'm glad Kim doesn't seem too interested in getting to know me, because it would be super weird if she started asking a bunch of questions like, "Where do you live?" or "What's your screen name?"

"Do my lips look plump?" Lexi demands now, pouting them out at us. She's put on two coats of lip plumper, and her lips look like Angelina Jolie's.

"Yes," I say honestly.

"I'm getting it," Lexi says, dropping it into her basket.

After we check out (Lexi spends $47.58, Kim

spends $63.24, and I spend $7.14), we still have an hour before Lexi's mom is supposed to pick us up.

"Should we DDR again?" I ask hopefully. I'm planning on taking my dad to DDR soon and I want to make sure I'm in top DDRing shape so I can impress him with my skills.

"I'm bored with DDR," Kim says, rolling her eyes.

"We could go to the bookstore and have a latte," Lexi offers.

"No," Kim says forcefully. "We're getting manicures." She marches off in the direction of the nail salon. Lexi and I look at each other, shrug, and then follow.

"Aren't you gonna get your nails done, Devi?" Lexi asks me once we're in the salon and she and Kim have picked out their nail polish (pink sparkles for Lexi and a bright yellow for Kim.) She takes a seat on one of the plush leather stools in the salon and hands the bottle of polish to the nail technician.

"I don't think so," I say, trying not to breathe through my nose. The salon doesn't smell very nice. It smells like chemicals.

"Why not?" Kim asks.

"I didn't bring enough money," I lie. I *do* have enough money left over, but I don't think my mom would be too pleased if I spent her money on a manicure. She gave me the money herself, out of the money her new business has made, and I know she was really proud that she was able to do that. So I'm not going to abuse it. Besides, she's going to look at the receipts. I know this because she said to me, "Make sure you bring me the receipts."

"So, anyway," Kim says to Lexi, "I didn't want to have to tell him, but there was no way he was going to be able to ask her out. I mean, she is soooo out of his league." She rolls her eyes.

I have no idea who or what Kim is talking about. Kim and Lexi are sitting at adjoining nail stations and I'm sitting on one of the hard plastic chairs in the waiting area, so it's kind of hard for me to join in the conversation. I consider pulling a chair up behind them so that I can hear them better, but I'm not sure if that would be lame or not. I pluck a *People* magazine off the stack on the table and pretend to be totally engrossed in an article about some country music singer I've never heard of.

"You did the right thing," Lexi tells Kim. "She *is* so totally out of his league, and you saved him a ton of embarrassment." Kim nods seriously. Who are they talking about? And how does Lexi know this? She's only been here a few days! Totally not enough time to be an expert on the social hierarchy of Robert Hawk Junior High. Plus she thinks Jared and I are together, so she's obviously not that good at picking out perfect matches.

"You okay over there, Devi?" Kim asks, raising her eyebrows and glancing over her shoulder.

"Of course," I say. I throw the *People* magazine down and pick up a book of hairstyles.

"Ooh, Devi, are you going to get your hair cut?" Lexi squeals. "That would be fab."

"No," I say. But then I remember that while Devon doesn't necessarily get her hair cut on a regular basis, Devi is probably always at the salon, getting her hair styled and cut. "Well, actually, yes, at some point. But not today."

"Why not?" Kim asks. "We have time. And besides, it's not like they're busy." She tilts her head toward the other side of the salon, where three hairdressers are standing around, seemingly with nothing to do.

"Not today," I say.

"Whatev." Kim shrugs her shoulders and turns back to Lexi. "Anyway, I think Jared likes you."

"What do you mean?" Lexi asks, frowning. Oh no, oh no, oh no. Okay, Devon. Don't panic. Remember what happens when you panic.

"I think he likes you," Kim repeats. "I can tell by the way he looks at you."

Don't panic, don't panic, don't panic. All I need is to get them off this topic. All I need is some kind of distraction. All I need is . . .

"I think I will get my hair cut after all!" I exclaim, jumping out of my chair and running over to where Kim and Lexi are sitting. I throw the book of hairstyles down on Lexi's nail station and start flipping through the pages like a madwoman. "What do you guys think? Bangs? Or maybe layers? How short? I don't think it should be too short, because I still want to be able to put it in a ponytail. Although a little off the bottom might be okay, because—"

"You," Kim declares, interrupting me, "need long layers. And some blond highlights around your face."

"Oh, no," I say, starting to get a weird feeling in my stomach. "No highlights, thanks. I only have sixty dollars." And my mom would disown me.

"I thought you didn't have any money," Kim says, blinking her sparkly eyes at me.

"I had more than I thought," I lie. "But highlights are going to be way more than that." Aren't they? I think highlights are around a hundred dollars. At least, that's what they always pay on TV for a decent color. I saw it on a *Sex and the City* rerun. Which I wasn't supposed to be watching.

"You just get the top done," Lexi says. "It's like fifty bucks and it doesn't take as long." She puts her hand in my face. "What do you think about this color? Is it too pink?"

"Um, I don't think so," I say.

"It totally is," Kim says.

"Hmm," Lexi puts her hand back down on the table. "I think I might want to change my color." The nail technician nods and pulls out a bunch of tiny bottles of polish. Lexi studies them critically.

"Excuse me!" Kim yells over to the hairdressers on the other side of the room. One of them, a very tall woman with black hair, comes rushing over. Her nametag says, LUCINDA. "Hi," Kim goes on. "My friend here"—she points to me—"would like to get her hair cut and some blond highlights, just around the top."

"Certainly," Lucinda says, all businesslike. "Come with me." She produces some sort of black cape as if she's a magician and ties it around my shoulders.

"Actually," I start to say, "I'm not—"

"And a shampoo, too, please," Kim calls after us. I see Lexi nod in agreement.

Lucinda plops me down in a chair, leans my head

back and, before I can protest, starts running warm water over my hair. I want to tell her to stop, but it feels too good. Nothing like when I get my hair cut at the Hairport near my house. Lucinda pulls a bottle of yummy-smelling shampoo off the shelf over my head and starts rubbing it into my scalp. Mmm. Relaxing. Maybe I'll just take the shampoo and then I can tell her I changed my mind. Yes, that's what I'll do. I'm already in the middle of getting my hair washed, anyway, so it's not like I can stop her. That would be rude, pulling up my big, soapy head. Not to mention a total mess. I'll just take the shampoo and then tell her. Mmm. Feels good. But I'm definitely stopping. Really, I am.

An hour later, I leave the salon with a newly shaped haircut, blond highlights, and no money.

"Devon Nicole Delaney!" To say my mom is not pleased with my new look would be putting it mildly. "We're going back. You're getting it fixed." She grabs her keys and her wallet off the counter and turns to Katie, who's sitting on the living room couch. "Katie, get dressed. We're going to the mall."

"The mall, the mall, the mall," Katie sings. She stands up and twirls around. "I love the mall. And I am dressed."

"Then get your shoes on." Katie runs off.

"Mom, this is not a big deal," I say, trying to sound mature in an effort to deal with her reasonably. "It's just a few highlights." I am in love with my new haircut. Seriously, I don't know why anyone would get an extreme makeover when they can just go to Lucinda. I feel like a whole new person. Which is a strange choice of words, given the fact that I've been living someone else's life. But maybe this is the life I was supposed to lead. Maybe I was supposed to be A-list this whole time and I just needed an excuse to let the new, better Devon out. Like those people who lose a ton of weight and then claim their new thin selves are the person they were supposed to be. You'd think my mom would realize this because she watches so much *Oprah*.

"A few highlights that you got without my permission and with my money," she says, throwing her hands up in the air. Hmm. My mom could seriously use a manicure.

"If it's the money, I'll pay you back," I say. "I'll babysit Katie, whatever you want."

"That's not the point, Devon," my mom says. She yanks a blue-and-white sneaker onto her foot and starts tying her laces.

"Mom," I say, putting my hand over hers and

stopping her from tying. "Please. Calm. Down. It's just some hair dye." She sighs. "Listen, can we talk about this later? After we've both cooled down? I'm sorry I didn't ask permission, but if I knew you were going to get this upset about it, I definitely would have." My mom doesn't say anything, and I rush on. "Plus Luke is going to be here any minute to work on our project."

Our doorbell rings then, saving me like a snow-storm on the day of a big test.

"Fine," my mom fumes. She pulls her sneaker off. She still looks very, very mad. "But we will be dealing with this later."

"I know," I say seriously. I race to the door. Luke's standing there, wearing a blue-and-white sweater and eating an apple. His green book bag is slung over his shoulder. "What's up?"

"Hey," I say, holding the door as he slides by me. Is Luke wearing cologne? He smells . . . different. I sniff the air around him experimentally.

"You changed your hair," he says as I shut the door.

"Oh," I say. "Yeah, I just got it done."

"It looks nice," he says, and I feel myself flushing. He bends down to take his shoes off (so polite!), and

I catch a whiff of what could be cologne again. Sniff, sniff. Still can't tell. Maybe he just smells like a boy. I'm not usually close enough to any boys to know what they smell like.

"Thanks."

"You're welcome." He smiles.

"So where do you want to work?" I ask. "We could do it in here, I guess, or—"

"I'm ready for the mall!" Katie announces, bursting into the room. She's in normal (read: non-Olympian) clothes for once. A pair of jeans and a pink and white polka-dotted sweater. "Oh," she says when she sees Luke. "Hello."

"Hi," Luke says.

"We're not going to the mall anymore," I say. "So you can go in the kitchen. We're going to be working on our project in the living room."

"Okay," Katie says, shrugging. Her blue eyes stay fixated on Luke. "I forget your name."

"It's Luke," he says. "And you're Katie, right?"

"Are you Devon's boyfriend?" Katie asks seriously, ignoring his question. Uh-oh. Danger, Will Robinson. Who is Will Robinson, anyway? I think he's a pilot.

"No," I say. I put my hands firmly on Katie's shoulders and start to push her toward the kitchen. "He's not

my boyfriend. We're working together on a very important project for school. Some *homework*." I emphasize
the word "homework" since, for some reason, Katie
gets scared by it. It seems super serious to her.

"Okay," Katie agrees as I propel her toward the
door. "I forgot your boyfriend's name is Jarrreeeeeddd."
Katie squeals and then goes running into the kitchen.

"Sorry about that," I say to Luke. "She's a kid, you
know." I roll my eyes, hoping he'll accept that excuse
for Katie's obvious insanity.

"You like Jared?" Luke asks, sounding surprised.
Probably because (a) up until a few days ago, I'd never
even really conversed with Jared, and (b) Luke is Jared's
best friend, and knows I definitely don't have a chance
with him.

"Jared who?" I ask, trying to play cool.

Luke frowns.

"Oh, Jared Bentley," I say, backpedaling. "No, I
don't like him. Katie thinks that any guy I hang out
with is my boyfriend." He looks skeptical. "She's five,"
I explain.

"Right," he says, sitting down on the couch. He
slides his bag over his shoulder and unzips it, pulling
out a bunch of papers. "So I was thinking it would
be a good idea to have the script pretty much nailed

down tonight so that everyone will have enough time to memorize their parts before Saturday."

"Good idea," I say. "Let me show you the outline I came up with. Be right back." I run to my room and pull out the outline I worked on earlier in study hall. It has all the important players of the Declaration of Independence, including some ideas for what I think they could say, some debates they could have, and who I think would be good for what parts. (I gave me and Luke the biggest parts since it's our project and Lexi and Kim the smallest since I have a hard time believing they're going to take this seriously.)

"Devon, this is great," Luke says once he reads it. "Seriously, this is really awesome."

"Really?" I say, flushing from the compliment.

"Yeah, this is going to make it a lot easier to get everything done. You've done most of the work."

"Oh, hello," my mom says, coming into the room. Oh, geez. "You must be Luke."

"Yes," Luke says, standing up. "It's nice to meet you, Mrs. Delaney." He holds his hand out, and they shake.

"Just popping in to see if you two need anything," my mom says, trying to sound innocent.

"No," I say. "We're fine."

"Okay," she says breezily. "I'll be right in the kitchen if you do." She emphasizes the words "right in the kitchen" I think in an effort to point out how close she'll be to where we are.

"Sorry about that," I say once my mom is out of earshot. "She's totally overprotective."

"It's cool," Luke says. "My dad's the same way. Whenever I'm at his house, he checks on me every five minutes. I can't be on the computer or the phone past eight, and if I want to go anywhere, I have to let him know, like, five days in advance." He rolls his eyes.

"Your parents are divorced?"

"Yup," he says, like it's no big deal. "But it's cool. I see my dad a lot. Even though he's kind of a pain." He grins.

"Yeah," I say. "Same with my mom. I know she only does it because she cares, but it's still kind of annoying. Like, she flipped out when she saw my hair."

"Really?" Luke asks. "Isn't it funny the stuff they get upset about? I mean, it's just a little hair dye." He reaches over and pulls my hair, as if to prove his point.

"That's exactly what I said!" I tell him. "Yet they have no problem with me going to school, where tons more dangerous things can happen."

"My dad's definitely been worse since the divorce,"

Luke says. "It's like he wants to make sure he's still a good dad, so he does it by being more protective."

I pause for a second, wondering how much to reveal. "Same with my parents," I say finally. I look down at my hands. "This past summer they were thinking about separating."

"That sucks," he says, looking serious. He looks at me and doesn't say anything, which is nice. I hate when you tell someone something important and they start asking a bunch of weird questions.

"They're okay now," I say. "They're working it out. But I think that's why she's being a little more protective lately."

"That makes sense," Luke says. "She wants to make sure she's being good to her family."

I flush, realizing that not only am I having a real conversation with a boy, but that Luke's now the only one besides Lexi who knows about my parents. I like the way he's so cool about it, like how he knows that what goes on in our parents' relationship has nothing to do with us. It seems so grown up.

We spend the next two hours going over the script, getting it ready to give to everyone to memorize. My mom comes into the living room from the kitchen about a hundred times. ("Do you think it's too cold in here?" "Did you remember to feed the cat?") It's kind of annoying, but I smile and answer her questions in an effort to distract her from the fact that she's mad at me. Plus, every time she does, Luke gives me this secret smile, which is kind of nice.

"So I'll make copies for everyone in the morning," Luke says when we're done. "And we'll hand them out at lunch tomorrow."

"Oh," my mom says, coming into the room. Again. "Are you guys finished?"

"Yes, Mrs. Delaney," Luke says, zipping up his backpack. "Thanks to your daughter and her amazing outline."

I blush again.

"I'll talk to you in school tomorrow," I say to Luke. I need to get him out of here before my mom or Katie says something uber-embarrassing.

"So," my mom says once Luke shuts the front door behind him. "I've thought about it, and I've decided you can keep the hair."

"Thank you, thank you, thank you," I say, rushing over to her and grabbing her in a hug.

"If," she says, disentangling herself from my grasp, "you promise to pay for it. You can start by babysitting Katie on Saturday night. Your father and I are going out." She smoothes her hair back, and I can tell this time "going out" means "going out" on a date. I've never heard of Saturday night therapy appointments.

"Okay," I say. "But I'm going to Jared's to work on my project at two o'clock."

"We're not going out until seven," she says. "So you should have plenty of time."

"Perfect," I say. I don't even mind babysitting Katie. Anything that allows my parents to spend time together is fine with me. Besides, it'll be fun. Katie and I can make cookies or something. I give my mom a kiss on the cheek and then head to the kitchen for dinner, my new hair bouncing behind me.

"Oh," Mel says when she sees me at school the next morning. "You did something to your hair."

"Yup," I say, doing a twirl in the hall. "I got it cut. And highlighted." I'm also wearing a new pair of jeans with a pink-and-maroon striped hooded sweater. I feel fab.

"Oh." Silence.

"Do you like it?"

"It's okay." She looks at the ground and shifts her bag to her other arm. "Here." She thrusts our notebook at me, hitting me in the stomach with the binding. All right then.

"What did you do last night?" I ask, taking the notebook and putting it in my locker. I glance down the hall nervously. I see Jared at his locker, stuffing some papers into his bag. Wow, he looks really unorganized. No wonder he's always having trouble in English. That boy needs a planner. Or at least a folder. Lexi is nowhere to be seen. I relax slightly.

"Homework," Mel says, sounding short. "I called you, but you never called me back. And your away message was up all night."

"Yeah, I was at the mall and then later, Luke came over to work on our project." I know I shouldn't feel guilty for hanging out with Lexi and working on my project with Luke, but for some reason I do. Maybe it's because I know I haven't been paying as much attention to Mel as I should have been these last few days. Or maybe it's because last night I told Luke about my parents, when I still haven't told Mel.

"Okay," Mel says, not really sounding like it is.

"Are you mad?" I ask. I feel a lump in my throat.

"No," she says, sighing. "I just feel like you haven't really had time for me the past couple of days, you know? You never call me back, and you forgot about meeting me twice."

"I know," I say, trying to swallow around the lump. "I'm so sorry. It's just been crazy with everything that's going on. But it's only going to be for a little while longer, and then I'll stage the fake breakup and everything will go back to normal, you'll see."

"I guess," Mel says, not sounding convinced.

"Hey, listen," I say, "do you want to be in the skit Luke and I are doing for our history project? We're going to work on it at lunch."

"I can't," Mel says. "I have to make up a test during lunch, so I won't be around." She looks at the ground.

"Oh." I try again. "Well, do you want to hang out later?" I ask. "I could come over, we could watch On Demand movies or something. And we could talk about the whole Brent-saying-hi-to-you-in-the-library situation."

"Okay," Mel says, brightening. "And we can do our homework together and order pizza."

"Fab," I say. "And I'll try to find the *CosmoGIRL!* article that talks about the head nod and what it means."

Later, in English, I'm in my seat, waiting for class to start, when Kim comes in and plops down in the seat ahead of me, the seat where Jared usually sits.

"Your hair," she declares, "looks fabulous." Must be Nice Kim I'm dealing with right now. Thank God. I'm not in the right mental state to deal with her other personality, Mean Girl Kim.

"Thanks," I say, giving it a shake. Love that Lucinda.

"So tell me what it was about," she says, tilting her head and looking at me seriously.

"Tell you what what was about?" I ask, wondering if I'm out of the loop again.

"The assignment," she says, rolling her eyes. "Whatever it was we were supposed to read." Today she has pink sparkles on her eyes to match the pink V-neck sweater and matching pink pants she's wearing. She looks like a big batch of cotton candy.

"Oh," I say. "Um, we didn't have to read anything for today." Did we? I pull out my assignment book, suddenly panicked. Is it possible that in all my new-haircut excitement I forgot an assignment?

"Oh, thank goodness," she says. "I always forget to do the reading assignments." Is she serious? The reading assignments are, like, the basis of the class.

"Yeah," I say doubtfully.

"So what's up for the weekend?" she asks. "Luke

said we're all doing your little play." She rolls her eyes like she can't believe the ridiculousness of us doing a play. It's not like we had a choice. It's a school assignment. Although maybe in Kim's world, school assignments are optional. "But seeing Luke in a costume is definitely worth giving up my Saturday."

Whoa. Does Kim like Luke? For some reason, this idea bothers me. I don't know why. If Kim likes Luke, then I don't have to worry about her liking Jared. How would Devi handle this? "Kim, do you like Luke?" I ask, trying to sound playful and Devi-like.

"Why?" she asks, her eyes narrowing. "What did you hear?"

Yikes. The last thing I need is Kim being mad at me. "Oh, um, nothing," I say. Time to change the subject. "So listen." I lean forward so no one else can hear us.

"Remember what you said yesterday? About Jared liking Lexi?"

"Isn't that so cute?" she says loudly. "They would be the cutest couple. Don't you think?"

"Yeah." No. "Anyway, just out of curiosity, why do you think he likes her?"

"Who? Jared?"

No, Prince William. "Yeah," I say. I twirl a strand

of my newly cut hair around my finger and hope I look and sound casual.

"Because he told me," she says, shrugging.

Must. Not. Panic. "What did he say?"

"What do you mean, what did he say? He said, 'I like Lexi.'"

"Hey," Jared says, walking up to his seat. He looks at Kim. "You're in my seat."

"So?" Kim says. "I'm talking to Devi."

"But it's my seat." He sets his books down on his desk. They're covered in *Star Wars* book covers, which I've never noticed until just now. *Star Wars*. Weird. I've never gotten that whole *Star Wars* fascination some people have. My dad loves those movies. He's always trying to get me to watch them with him, but Darth Vader scares me. Plus everyone knows the line "Luke, I am your father," which is like the big surprise ending, and it kind of kills the movie if you already know that when you start watching.

"It's not really your seat until the bell rings," Kim says. "Until then, it's whoever gets here first." Jared reaches out and grabs Kim around the waist and starts tickling her. She giggles and throws her head back, her hair making a blond river down her back.

"Jared, stop," she says. She tries to block his hands,

but he's stronger than her. How awkward. Sitting here while they flirt. La, la, la. Why is Jared being so flirty with Kim if he likes Lexi, anyway?

"Okay, okay," Kim says, holding up her hands in surrender. "You can have your seat back." She flounces off in a haze of sparkles and perfume. Kim apparently also thinks saying good-bye is optional.

"Whaddup?" Jared asks me.

"Not much," I say. My mouth feels like it's been stuffed with cotton.

"Did you do something to your hair?" He frowns. "You look . . ." Hot? Beautiful? Gorgeous? " . . . different."

"Yeah," I say, talking through my cottonmouth. "I got it highlighted."

"Cool." He turns back around, and I stare at the back of his neck. Smooth. Tan. I have to resist the urge to reach out and touch it. I debate whether or not I should try to do damage control for the weekend. If I don't, I risk Jared flirting with Lexi. If I do, I actually have to initiate conversation with Jared, which is still hard for me. I take a deep breath.

"So, um, Jared?" I ask, figuring overcoming my nervousness around Jared is an integral part of not getting caught in all my lies.

"Yeah?" he asks, turning back around. His eyes are really blue. I take another deep breath. I can do this. It's just like playing a role. I try to turn into Devi.

"Um, did you tell Kim that you had a thing for Lexi?"

"Yeah," he says. He turns back around toward the front of the classroom. What is with these people? Acting totally casual about things that are obviously HUGE DEALS?

"How come?" I persist.

"How come what?" he asks, sighing. He seems annoyed.

"How come you told Kim you have a thing for Lexi?" I repeat, trying to keep my tone light.

"Because I do." This conversation is beginning to feel like a merry-go-round. It's moving, but it's definitely not going anywhere. I decide to try a different tactic.

"Right, but remember how I told you that Lexi doesn't like guys to fall all over her?"

"That's not really falling all over her." He leans over the back of his seat then, like he wants to tell me a secret, and I lean in to meet him halfway. "If you want to know the truth . . ." He trails off and looks around to make sure no one is listening. I'm so close, I can feel his breath against my face. It smells like peppermint.

Probably because he's always chewing gum in school, even though we're not supposed to. "I've been kind of mean to her."

"You've been mean to her?" I wonder what it would be like to kiss him. His lips look soft, like two plump pink pillows. Wait. If I'm this close to him, that means he's that close to me. I suddenly feel self-conscious about my lips. I hope they look kissable.

"Oh, yeah," he says, looking almost proud. "The other day when we were walking out of school, I completely ignored her."

"Great!" I say. "That's the way to go, seriously." I wonder if I can discreetly reach into the bag by my feet and pull out the lip gloss I got at Sephora yesterday.

"You're definitely right," he says, nodding. His face is still mere inches from mine. I start reaching toward my bag slowly with my right hand.

"I am?" Stretch. Reach.

"Yeah," Jared says, leaning in even farther. "It's like when I saw her with Matt yesterday in the cafeteria. He was all over her, and she didn't seem into him at all."

"Exactly," I say, nodding. My fingers brush against my bag. I reach my hand in and try to grope around discreetly for my lip gloss. Keys, pink wallet with nothing in it (thanks to yesterday's big shopping spree), gum, a CD of stuff I downloaded illegally off of Limewire, a jump drive that has the draft of the script for my project with Luke . . . I'm touching everything but my lip gloss. Why do I have so much stuff in here, anyway? Eww, what is that? A tissue? I hope it's not used. My palm touches the tube of gloss. Finally.

"It's not that hard, actually," Jared says, shrugging.

"What isn't that hard?" I uncap the tube of gloss and get ready to smear some on, drawing attention to my lips, thereby drawing attention to the fact that I'm kissable, thereby making Jared want to kiss me.

"To be mean to her." He shrugs again. "I dunno why. I just pretend she's anyone, like any random girl. Like you or someone else. Not Lexi."

"Oh." I know he didn't say it to be mean, but still. He turns back around then, toward the front of the classroom, before I have a chance to put on my lip gloss and make my lips kissable.

"What do you want on your pizza?" Mel asks later that afternoon. We're in her room, trying to pick out a movie to watch. Mel has more than three hundred DVDs. Every time her parents go to the video store to get a new documentary, they let Mel pick out DVDs from the used DVD bin. She hasn't even gotten around to watching some of them.

"Pepperoni," I say, scanning the huge rack of movies. Hmm. Something that's not too depressing.

Mel calls to her mom, who appears at her bedroom door as if by magic. "Mom, can you order us a pizza, half pepperoni and half green pepper and onions?" Mel and her family are vegetarians, which always makes me feel a little weird, having meat in their house. They don't seem to mind, but still.

"Sure," Mel's mom says. "How are you, Devon?"

Oh, great. I'm just a big liar, though. "I'm great," I say.

"Melissa, please make sure you take your laundry down later tonight," Mel's mom says.

"I will," Mel says. Her mom leaves to go order the pizza, and Mel crosses the room to her hamper, pulls out her dirty clothes, and drops them into a laundry basket. "Today's laundry day," she explains.

"Right," I say. We don't have laundry day at my house. Although my mom (and my dad) have been way better lately about doing chores around the house, we definitely don't have a specific day dedicated to laundry. We just kind of wait until our hampers are full.

"How was lunch?" Mel asks.

"It was okay," I say. "We're going to practice the skit tomorrow at Jared's if you want to come." Luke and I spent most of our lunch period going over the script with everyone, and I realize now that since Mel was making up her test, I didn't think to assign her a part. At the time, I didn't even realize Mel wasn't there. I was distracted. Matt O'Connor kept flirting with Lexi, and Lexi was flirting back. Plus Kim kept yelling about how she didn't have enough lines, and if she was going to give up her Saturday to work on some dumb project that she wasn't even being graded on, someone better give her a bigger part. But I'm sure I can work Mel into the script somewhere. Or she can hold cue cards or something.

I pull *Sixteen Candles* out of Mel's DVD collection and throw it on the bed. "I want to watch this," I say.

"Again?" Mel asks, rolling her eyes.

"Yes, again," I say. *Sixteen Candles* is this really great movie about a girl named Sam. Her whole family forgets her sixteenth birthday, but it turns out okay because the hottest guy in school, Jake Ryan, ends up falling in love with her, even though she's a sophomore and he's a senior and he pretty much didn't know she was alive until he decided he wanted more than his ditzy blond girlfriend. It is a very good movie.

"Fine," Mel says. She crosses the room and plops down on the bed. "But first show me the *CosmoGIRL!* article."

I pull the magazine from my bag and show her the article, which is called, "Hello There! How to Use His Body Language to Decipher Exactly What His Greeting Means."

"Read it," Mel instructs.

"'A nod accompanied by a hi can mean one of two things,'" I recite. "'If he nods down toward you, it's a friendly, you're like my bud kind of hi. But if he tilts his chin upward, it means he sees you as someone he wants to flirt with, and possibly more.'"

Mel squeals. "Do you think it's true?"

"Of course it's true," I say. "They quote a body language expert and everything." How does one get to be a body language expert, anyway? Do you need a college degree, or is it just like a course you can take? Because that skill could really come in handy.

"So what does it say to do?" Mel asks.

"It doesn't," I say.

"Then what good is it?"

"Well, you have to build upon it," I say. "For example, now we can move on to this article, about if you should make the first move or not."

"Okay." Mel nods.

"Oh, good, it has a quiz." I clear my throat. "'Number one. If you're in a class with your crush, he (a) ignores you, (b) says hi, (c) spends the whole period talking to you.'"

"Um, *a*," Mel says. "Brent ignores me in class."

"Are you sure?" I ask. "He doesn't say anything to you?"

"Not really," Mel asks. "Sometimes he asks me for answers."

Hmmm. I mark down *a*. This isn't looking good.

"Next question. 'If you saw him outside of school hours, he would most likely (a) say hi to you, (b) ignore you, (c) introduce his friends to you.'"

"*B*," Mel says. "He would ignore me."

"Mel!" I say. "He said hi to you in the library."

"That was in school," she points out. "And the question says 'outside of school hours.'"

We take the rest of the quiz, tally up her score, and then Mel reads the result. "'This guy knows who you are, but if you want something to happen, you're going to have to do it yourself. Watch out, though—it doesn't seem like you're on his radar. So be careful about setting yourself up for a disappointment. You may want to wait until you he gives you some kind of sign.'" Mel frowns. "So basically it's telling me I have to make the first move, but that if I do, it's going to be a disaster."

"Not necessarily," I say quickly, not wanting her to feel bad. "Plus it's just a dumb magazine." I throw it across the room.

"But what about the head nod?" she says. "The magazine said the head nod meant he was being flirty."

"Well, they were right about *that*," I say. "I mean, they had a body language expert."

Mel's mom knocks on the door then with the pizza, and we spend the rest of the afternoon watching DVDs and eating. By the time I get home, I'm exhausted and in a pizza coma. Thank God it's Friday and I don't have to worry about getting my homework done or waking up early tomorrow.

The house is quiet when I walk in, and I find my dad in the living room, flipping through the channels.

"Hey," I say, plopping down into the chair next to him. "Where is everyone?"

"Your mom went grocery shopping and she took Katie with her." He flips a little bit more, settles on a *Seinfeld* rerun, and then sets the remote on the coffee table. I start to feel a little worried. If my mom is out of the house with Katie, that may mean she wanted to get away from my dad.

"Hey," my dad says, seeing the expression on my face. "Relax." He laughs. "Everything's fine."

"Are you sure?" I ask, swallowing hard.

"I'm positive," he says. "They just went grocery shopping, that's all."

"And you would tell me if it wasn't, right?" I ask.

"Of course," he says. He looks me straight in the eye.

"Okay," I say. "I'm sorry if I'm being paranoid." Even though I knew my parents were fighting a lot, I never thought they were getting to the point where they were thinking about separating or even getting a divorce. So when they told Katie and me that we were going away for the summer, I felt kind of blindsided.

I can still remember the conversation. They pulled us into the kitchen, sat us down, and told us they were thinking about separating and needed time to themselves to figure things out. Katie immediately burst into tears. I almost did too, but I waited until later, when I was up in my room, thinking about how horrible it was going to be to have to be away from Mel and my parents for the summer. I remember how relieved I was when my parents decided to stay together. There's no way I want to go back to that feeling of not knowing what's going on.

He sighs and runs his hands through his hair. "I'm sure it seemed like the stuff that happened this summer was sudden," he says. "But it was really building up for a while. Your mother and I should have been more honest with you." I don't say anything. "But we've learned from our mistakes."

"Okay," I say. I start to get a little choked up, even though he's telling me everything is fine. I look down at my hands.

"Devon," he says. He reaches over and tilts my chin up so that I'm looking at him. "I promise I will always be honest with you about this stuff."

"Okay," I say, forcing a smile.

"Do you believe me?"

"Yes," I say, wondering what my dad would think if he knew I'd been lying to everyone about everything.

"Good," he says, standing up from the couch. "Now what do you say we make some popcorn and watch some trashy reality TV?"

"Hmm," I say, pretending to think about it. "Extra butter?"

"Sure."

"Extra butter and cheese?"

"Are you tryin' to give me a heart attack?" he jokes, clutching his chest and pretending to fall onto the couch. I giggle, then happily skip off to the kitchen with him.

chapter seven

"There's not a part for her, though,"
Lexi says on the phone later that night, when I bring up asking Mel to come to Jared's to work on the project.

"We could probably work one in," I say. "Or she could do the camera work."

"Matt's going to do the camera work," she points out.

"Well, maybe Mel could hold cue cards or something." Aren't there like five million people who work on movies? How can there not be one job for Mel?

"We're not having cue cards," Lexi says, sounding

exasperated with me. "Besides, I don't think it's such a good idea to have her there."

"Why not?"

"Well, first of all, it doesn't even really seem like she's friends with anyone except you." Uh-oh. "In fact, Kim hardly even knew her name." Lexi sighs.

"Well, she is definitely more like *my* friend," I say carefully. "She's not really close with anyone else in our group. She's shy."

"Plus," Lexi goes on, "I don't know if it's such a good idea that she's around Jared all the time. I think it just adds a lot of stress on your relationship."

"On whose relationship?"

"Yours and Jared's." It does?

"What makes you say that?"

"It just doesn't seem like you two are getting along lately." It doesn't?

"It doesn't?"

"No," she says. "He hardly even looks at you, and I think it's because Mel's always around." Actually, Mel's hardly ever around, and he hardly looks at me because he's not really my boyfriend. But I don't say this. Obviously. "Besides," she goes on. "Have you and Jared even hung out since we all went to the mall?"

Since we've gone to the mall? That was just a few days ago. I try to remember what I told Lexi over the summer about how often Jared and I hung out. I think it was a lot. Crap. I quickly try to come up with a time Jared and I have hung out that wouldn't conflict with a time I was hanging out with, IM'ing, or talking on the phone with Lexi. "Of course we've hung out," I say, deciding to leave it at that.

"When?" she asks. "When did you guys hang out?"

"Um, the day before yesterday."

"But didn't he have practice?"

"Practice for what?" I ask before I can think.

"Soccer practice," she says, sighing. "For his league!"

Jared plays on a league? "Um, we hung out after." I'm losing it. This is not good. And when did Lexi become so versed in knowing Jared's schedule, anyway?

"Well, whatever," Lexi says. "I'm just saying that it seems that when Mel's around, it definitely puts a strain on you guys. And like I said, it doesn't really seem like she's friends with anyone else."

"It's fine," I say. "It's not a big deal." I can just tell Mel that there's really no reason for her to go. Why should she give up her Saturday just to work on my stupid project?

"So what's the deal with you and Matt O'Connor?" I ask Lexi, anxious to change the subject.

"What do you mean?" Lexi asks, sounding excited that someone's noticed their flirtation.

"You guys have been all flirty and stuff in lunch," I say. "And he's pretty cute."

"He *is* really cute," Lexi agrees. "I'm going to ask him to hang out after we work on the project this weekend." I breathe a sigh of relief. If Lexi is interested in Matt, that means she doesn't like Jared. Which means I'm not keeping them apart. Which means I have nothing to feel bad about. Well, besides the fact that Jared's being mean to her for no reason. But she doesn't seem to care too much about that. Still, when I hang up the phone with Lexi and run off to my bedroom to look for something to wear to Jared's the next day, I have a bad feeling in my stomach. And I don't think it's from all the pizza and popcorn.

"Devon."

Zzzzz.

"Devonnnn!"

Mmmmm.

"DEVON!"

I open one eye slowly. Katie's nose is pressed up

against mine. She's staring at me, her eyes wide.

"What are you doing in here?" I ask, rolling over. I can see a faint amount of light through the blinds on the window by my bed, which means it's way too early to be awake. It's Saturday. Which means I get to sleep in as late as I want. Which means noon.

"I'm coming to get you," Katie says, jumping into bed with me.

"What time is it?" I ask. I hope she doesn't think I'm waking up to watch DVDs with her. Katie likes to get an early start on her day by watching DVDs. Over and over. The same movie, I mean. She picks one and keeps watching it until she knows it by heart.

"I think it's like . . ." she considers. "Ten o'clock." This could be true, or it could be grossly off the mark. Katie has trouble figuring out what time it is.

"Too early to get up," I say. She's quiet for a minute, and I start to drift back to sleep when she starts shaking me. "What?!"

"I came to get you," she says, sounding exasperated. "Because you have a phone call."

"Someone's on the phone for me?" I ask, pushing my sheets off. They tangle around my legs and almost make me trip. Katie giggles. Is it weird that I've created a whole new secret life for myself and yet I still think my sister may be crazier than me?

"Who is it?"

"I dunno." Katie shrugs. She pulls my covers over her head.

I run down the stairs and into the kitchen. My mom's at the stove, cooking scrambled eggs. The clock on the microwave says 10:02. I guess I didn't give Katie enough credit for her time-telling skills.

"Who's on the phone for me?" I ask, glancing at the phone in the kitchen, which is on the receiver.

"It was Luke," my mom says, pushing the eggs around the frying pan. She reaches up and pushes a strand of hair out of her face. "But you were taking so long to get to the phone, I told him you would call him back. Really, Devon, you have to be more aware of your bad sleep habits."

"I don't have bad sleep habits," I say. I pour myself a glass of orange juice and sit down at the table. "Did you get Luke's number?"

"Of course I got his number," my mom says, like the thought of her not getting it would be the same as her doing something totally crazy like shaving her head. She motions to the pad by the phone. "It's right there."

141

"Thanks," I say, gulping my juice.

"Do you want some eggs?" my mom asks. She doesn't wait for my answer before setting a plate of them in front of me.

"No thanks," I say, pushing them away. "I have to go call Luke back."

"Devon," she says, moving the plate away and sitting down next to me. Uh-oh. I can always tell when my mom is going to get all super serious on me. She uses my name a lot. Also, I've noticed that she likes to do it when I'm not expecting it. I think she learned this technique in the counseling she goes to with my dad, because one time I saw a brochure entitled *How to Talk to Your Kids About Anything* near her computer. I think the theory is that if it doesn't feel like a "planned talk," then it's more like two friends having a chat.

"Mom," I say, pushing the plate away and hoping I can run upstairs before we get into the talk. "I really have to call Luke back. We're getting together to work on our project today, and so . . ." I trail off, hoping she'll get the picture that, you know, working on the project is as important as world peace or something.

"I know," she says, nodding. "Which is why I want to have a quick talk with you before you go running off for the day." She folds her hands together.

"I just want you to know that it's normal at your age to like boys." Oh. My. God. My mom is not going to have a talk with me about boys. This is humiliating.

"I know," I say, nodding seriously and hoping my mom will understand that we don't need to have this talk because I'm so well adjusted and mature. If only she knew.

"So when boys call here, or when you want to hang out with boys, that's perfectly fine." She looks me in the eye and smiles. I smile back.

"Thanks, Mom," I say. "Good talk."

"But," she goes on, "there have to be some rules and limitations."

"Actually, there doesn't," I say, "because I'm not even really hanging out with any boys. Luke is just a friend, Mom. He called because of our project."

My mom raises her eyebrows at me, and I can tell she's wondering if she should press the issue or not. My mom is trying to set boundaries but also knows that she needs to give us space, too. "Room to make our own mistakes and grow from them." I read it in the brochure. Being a parent is horribly complicated.

Katie walks into the kitchen, her face smeared with makeup.

"Hello!" she announces. "I am here for my show." She gets up on the kitchen chair and starts dancing.

"That's your show?" I ask her. "I think it needs work."

"I am Katie Delaney, star of *The Katie Delaney Show*, and I am here to make you SHAKE YOUR BOOTY!" And then Katie does start shaking her booty.

"Katherine Grace Delaney, where did you hear that word?" my mom gasps, horrified. "And where did you get that makeup?" She looks over at me like I'm responsible for turning my sister into a five-year-old pop star.

"What word?" Katie asks. She puts her hands up in the air and continues to shake. "Now raise the roof! RAISE! THE! ROOF!"

"Hmm," I say. "That's actually not bad. Katie, you're a pretty good dancer."

"Thank you, Devon," Katie says. She continues to raise the roof.

"Devon, don't encourage her," my mom says. She stands up and lifts Katie off the chair. "You have makeup all over." She rips a paper towel off the holder by the sink, runs it under the faucet, and starts cleaning Katie's face. "Where did you get this makeup?"

"From Devon's room," Katie says. She turns and looks at me. "I'm sorry, Devon," she says solemnly. Katie has been big on apologizing ever since she learned about saying sorry in preschool last year. The problem is, she thinks once she's apologizes, it makes whatever she did totally okay.

"That's okay," I say. I don't mind that she took my makeup. From the looks of it, it's the sample lipstick that came with the lip gloss I bought while I was with Lexi and Kim. It's this horrible orange color. Plus I'm so grateful Katie distracted my mom from her "setting boundaries with boys" talk that I can't be mad.

"It's not okay," my mom says. "She has it all over!"

"Just put the clothes in the washing machine right away," I tell her. "And put some of that Stain Stick on it. I bet it will come out."

"Hmm," my mom says, looking at Katie, who grins. "Maybe you're right. Into the laundry room," she commands, and Katie marches off obediently.

The phone rings, and I grab the cordless off the counter.

"Hello?"

"Devi? It's Lexi."

"Hey," I say. "What's goin' on?" I grab the carton of orange juice off the table and refill my glass.

"Listen, something bad just happened." Geez. I'm putting out fires all over the place.

"Like what?" The juice hits the top of the glass and threatens to spill over. I take a small sip.

"Listen, before I tell you, you have to promise not to get mad." Uh-oh.

"Why would I be mad?" I set the container of orange juice back on the table.

"Do you promise?"

"Yes, I promise."

"I accidentally told Kim that Jared was your boy-friend."

"What do you mean?" I ask as my stomach drops.

"She told her!" I scream. I'm in my room, recounting the conversation I just had with Lexi to Mel, who rushed over after I called her freaking out.

"Okay," Mel says, sighing. She's perched on my bed, and I'm pacing the floor in front of her, back and forth, back and forth. I'm afraid if I sit down, I might explode. "And what did Kim say?"

"She didn't refute it. She just said 'that's interest-ing.' 'That's interesting'! What does that mean?" Mel looks at me blankly, and I grab her by the shoulders. "WHAT DOES THAT MEAN?" I demand.

Mel reaches up slowly, grabs my wrists, and pulls my hands off her shoulders. "Devon," she says. "You. Are. On. The. Brink."

She's right. "You're right," I say. DO. NOT. PANIC. I feel like I should have that tattooed somewhere on my body so that I can look at it whenever I need to. It's becoming almost like a motto. There should be a series of posters. "Someone choking? DO. NOT. PANIC." "Is your child lost in the mall? DO. NOT. PANIC." "About to have your secret life exposed and your life ruined? DO. NOT. PANIC."

"I just don't know what to do. This is a disaster."

"Maybe this isn't the right time to say this," Mel says slowly. "But, Devon, what did you expect to happen? The longer this goes on, the more chance there is that it's going to start causing problems."

"Gee, thanks," I say. I plop down on the bed next to her and sigh.

"I'm sorry, Devon, but it's true. You have to fake break up with him."

"I can't now!" I say. "It will definitely look fake if I break up with him right after Lexi told Kim. She'll know it was all a lie. Unless . . ." Suddenly I have a brilliant idea. "What if I can convince Kim that I'm dating Jared and that *she* has to keep it a secret too?"

"It won't work," Mel says, sighing.

"Why not?" I frown. "It's working with Lexi."

"It's *not* working with Lexi," Mel says. "And besides, that's different. Lexi and Jared aren't friends the way Kim and Jared are. Kim knows stuff about Jared, about his schedule and what he spends his time doing. She's not going to believe that you two are having a secret relationship. She knows that, before a few days ago, you two hardly even spoke."

"You're right," I moan, grabbing one of my pillows and pulling it over my head. "I'm in deep trouble. I'm done. Finished." I wonder if my mom will let me switch schools. Maybe to an all-girls school, since she's now convinced that I'm boy-crazy.

"You're not," Mel says. She slides down on the bed next to me. "Look, talk to Kim. Maybe you can explain the situation to her, find out what she thinks. Maybe she didn't even hear what Lexi said."

"Right," I say, not believing it. I'm doomed. Kids in future classes will talk about me. I'll be Devon Delaney, the girl who made up a fake boyfriend. People will probably think I'm an urban legend, since no one is going to believe that anyone could actually be that stupid.

"Look, nothing bad has happened yet," Mel says. She takes the pillow I'm holding over my face and moves it to the top of my bed. "Kim didn't tell Lexi the truth. So be thankful for that. You can't figure out what to do right now, because you don't know exactly what's going on. You have to take it one step at a time."

"You're right," I say. I take a deep breath. "But whatever it is can't be good."

"You'll know more about the situation in a little while," Mel asks, looking at me. "We're still going to Jared's to work on the project, right?"

"Actually, um, I meant to talk to you about that," I say, swallowing. "Um, it turns out that since you weren't at lunch, you didn't get a part."

"That's okay," Mel says, shrugging. "It will probably be more fun to just hang out there, anyway, and not have to worry about doing the work. Maybe I can help with the camera or something."

Crap. "Well," I say, "I think that Matt O'Connor's going to do the camera." Silence. This is bad. This is horrible.

"Oh," Mel says, looking down at her hands. "Well, whatever." She shrugs, but I can tell she's upset. "Maybe we can hang out later tonight. You're not going to be there all day, are you?"

"No," I say. "It's only going to take a couple of hours, but I have to babysit Katie tonight."

"Right," she says, standing up. "Maybe tomorrow then."

"Yes," I say, nodding. "Definitely tomorrow. Call me or IM me tonight. I'll be around."

"Okay," she says. "Have fun working on your project. Good luck with the Kim thing." She turns and walks out the door, her hair bobbing up and down, and suddenly I feel like I'm going to cry.

By the time I have to leave for Jared's, I'm definitely past being on the brink. I've crossed over into full-blown panic.

Possible openers:

"Hi, Kim, I heard you found out I'm a liar. Is there anything to drink around here?"

"Hey, Kim, just so you know, I really am dating Jared. Yes, I know it seems impossible since you two are such good friends and talk all the time, but I guess you weren't as close as you thought. SUCKER!"

"Kim, I'll do whatever you want, just please, please, please, don't tell anyone."

The third one is probably the most accurate. Although a combo of the first and third might work as well, because I really am thirsty.

Jared lives less than two blocks from me (which is actually very cool, since all last year Mel and I would walk by his house over and over, pretending we were just going for walks, and sometimes we'd see him outside fixing his bike or doing something in the yard for his mom), so I walk to his house, even though I'm wearing a pair of Lexi's shoes that are killing my feet. I wore sneakers out of the house and ditched them in the bushes, because I knew there was no way my mom was going to let me out of the house with these on my feet. Especially after her whole talk about boys. But the shoes are glam—pink with a chunky heel. Although Lexi's feet are a size bigger than mine, which means (a) the shoes make a scraping noise while I walk, and (b) I had to stuff toilet paper into the toes so that they wouldn't slide off.

I ring Jared's doorbell and plaster a smile on my face.

"Hey," he says when he answers the door. "Everyone's downstairs." Everyone's downstairs? What? I check my watch, which says 2:07. You'd think everyone would try to be fashionably late, but I guess not.

"Cool," I say. "Um, am I late or something?"

"I dunno," he says. He shrugs again, and I follow him

down the stairs to the basement. My shoes are clunking very loudly, and I'm trying to walk slowly in an effort not to bring attention to myself. Suddenly I have a horrible thought. What if Kim already asked Jared about me, and now *everyone knows*? And when I get down there, everyone's going to start yelling at me or something? Like in that old movie *Carrie*, where everyone plays a mean prank on the dorky girl at the end. Kind of like a surprise party. Only a very, very bad one.

But when I get into the basement, it doesn't seem like anything's about to go down. Lexi and Kim are in the corner, huddled over an iPod, picking out music, which is blaring out of the speakers all over the room. Luke's sitting on an overstuffed couch watching something on TV with Matt O'Connor. Jared wanders over and plops down next to them. Hmm. This looks more like a party than a school project.

I stand awkwardly at the bottom of the stairs for a second, wondering what I should do.

"Hey," Luke says, saving me. He gets up from the couch and comes over to where I'm standing. "We were waiting until you got here to start."

"I'm sorry if I'm late," I say. "Something, um, came up at home and I had to deal with it before I left."

He frowns, his eyes serious. "Is everything okay?"

Not really, I lied about going out with your best friend and now Kim knows about it, so I'm probably going to become the laughingstock of the school. "Yeah, everything's fine." I put on my most dazzling smile. Okay, new plan: I'm not going down without a fight.

I muster up all my courage, then walk over to the couch determinedly and sit down between Jared and Matt. "So," I say, trying to sound demure. "What are we watching?" I pull the remote out of Jared's hand, surprising myself. I didn't know I had that in me. Although I really have been doing a lot of Devi-like things lately. What if I lose Devon and become Devi? This is a disturbing thought.

"The game," Jared says, his eyes not moving from the screen.

"Great," I say. "I love the game." What sort of game? I wonder, peering at the screen. Looks like football.

"Hey, Lexi," Matt yells. "Can you play something good, please?"

"This *is* good!" Lexi giggles. "I want to listen to stuff you can dance to."

"Let me find something," Matt says. He gets up and heads over to where Lexi and Kim are.

"Nooo," Lexi squeals, but you can tell she likes the attention.

Luke sits down on the other side of me. "So you never called me back this morning," he says. "I was going to see if you wanted to get together for a little while and go over the script."

"I know, I'm sorry," I say. "But I was dealing with, uh, that thing I told you about before." Way to keep it vague.

"I understand," he says, nodding. Suddenly I'm very aware that Luke's hand is extremely close to mine on the couch. In fact, our hands are almost touching. Should I yank my hand back? But what if I do, and he thinks I moved it because I was nervous about touching his hand? Which isn't a big deal. Touching hands with someone, I mean. It's just hands. People touch the hands of strangers all the time. Like at checkouts.

"Yes!" Jared screams, jumping up off the couch. On the screen, one of the football guys slams the ball into the ground and starts doing a little dance around the end of the field.

The motion of Jared jumping up from the couch jostles my hand a little bit, and now it is touching Luke's. I. Am. Touching. Luke's. Hand. A current of electricity moves its way up my hand. Which makes no sense. Because I like Jared, not Luke. Suddenly, I'm hyperaware of the way Luke smells. Exactly like the way he did that night he was at my house, when we were talking about our parents. He's not moving his hand. Why isn't he moving his hand? This is nuts. I like Jared, not Luke. So I'll just move my hand and everything will be okay. La, la, la. My hand is still there. For some reason, I am incapable of moving my hand.

"All right," Jared says, clicking off the TV. "Game over. Now I'm ready to work."

"Oh, okay," I say, jumping up. "Great. Me too. I'm ready, I mean. To work." Jared gives me a weird look.

"Finally," Lexi says, coming over to where we are. "Is the stupid game over?"

"It's not stupid," Jared says, rolling his eyes at her.

"It kind of is," Lexi says. She's wearing a pink skirt that hangs low on her hips, and a white T-shirt that says BABY DOLL on it in sparkly letters. Her hair is in two pigtails, her feet are bare, and her toenails painted a shell-pink color that sparkles even under the dim lighting of the basement. "All they do is tackle one another."

"They tackle one another because it's part of the game," Jared says, sighing. "But you wouldn't understand." Wow. Guess I didn't have to worry about

Jared and the whole playing-hard-to-get thing. Good for him.

"Whatever," Lexi says, rolling her eyes. Jared winks at me.

Lexi looks at me for the first time since I got there. "Hi, Devi!"

"Hey," I say warily, looking at Kim, who's still over in the corner, manning the music. Lexi must see my nervous look, because she grabs my sleeve and pulls me a few feet away, out of the earshot of the guys. "Listen, don't worry about the Kim thing." She bites her lip. "She said she's not going to say anything."

"She said that?" Suddenly, I feel nervous, like when you're in the dentist's waiting room, waiting to go in. Kim must know it's a lie. So there must be a reason she's agreeing not to tell anyone. My stomach is dropping faster than an amusement park ride.

"Yeah." Lexi squeezes my arm. "So don't worry about it."

"So, listen," Luke says. "I was thinking that today we could just go over the script, do a run-through. And then maybe next weekend we'll do the actual filming. We can work on getting the costumes this week."

"Oh," I say. "I thought we were going to do the whole thing today."

"Well, I don't think everyone's memorized their lines yet," Luke says. "And we don't have costumes."

"Right," I say. Great. I'm playing John Hancock and I stayed up late last night memorizing my lines. I thought we'd be doing the whole project today, which I guess makes no sense, because like Luke said, we don't have costumes. I wonder what they wore while signing the Declaration of Independence. Probably some kind of long black robe. And those white wigs with the curls.

"Are we doing this or not?" Kim asks, finally abandoning the iPod and coming over. I move closer to Jared, just in case Kim might actually believe the ridiculousness that he and I are together. "Because I don't want to be hanging out here all day. Some of us actually have lives." Well, la di da. I have a life. If you count babysitting Katie as having plans.

"Yeah, let's get started." Agreeing with her can only get me on her good side, right? She glances at me and then looks away.

"All right," Luke says. "Does everyone have their scripts? We'll do a quick run-through. And try to put some feeling in your voices so that it doesn't sound lame."

We spend the next two hours reading the script

through a bunch of times and working on memorizing our lines. It would have taken a lot less time except Jared keeps screwing up his lines and making us take breaks so that he can check the score of the game. (Apparently, another one started after the first one was over.) Also, Matt is taking his job as cameraman way too seriously, and keeps circling around the table, trying to set up angles for when we film. He also keeps pulling Lexi's hair every time he passes by her chair, and she squeals and pretends she's bothered by it.

"Hey, Devi, can I talk to you for a second?" Kim says to me as I'm gathering up my papers after we're done with the last read-through. It's the first time she's said anything to me all afternoon.

"Sure," I say, forcing a bright smile on my face. DO. NOT. PANIC. I glance nervously to where Jared's on the couch in front of the TV, and wonder if I could start some sort of fake fight with him that would be grounds for a breakup. Something like, "All you ever do is watch football! I'm through with this!" But then I realize Jared might be like, "Um, through with what?", which wouldn't work.

"What's up?" I ask Kim after she pulls me over to where the iPod is. It's been blasting some kind of dance mix the whole time we were working, which was kind of distracting.

"I know you told Lexi you're dating Jared," Kim says. She tilts her head to the side and looks at me thoughtfully.

"Oh," I say, not sure what to do. Deny? Admit to it? Try to convince her it's true? Run?

"I also know you told her you were friends with all of us before she got here." She holds her hand out in front of her and studies her nails.

"Listen, Kim—"

She puts her hand up and silences me. "I'm not going to say anything," she says. She studies me.

"But I just wanted to let you know that I know." She leans in closer, and I can feel her breath on my cheek. "I think it's really mean that you lied to Lexi. And I haven't decided exactly what I'm going to do about it yet."

Lovely.

Luke insists on walking me home, which is horrible, because I feel like I'm going to cry. Plus my shoes are killing my feet, and I planned on walking home barefoot if I had to, but obviously I can't do that now.

What would I say? "Hi, can you hold my shoes while I walk home barefoot? Oh, don't worry about that. That's just some toilet paper I stuffed in the toes so that they would fit me."

"Sorry about Jared screwing up all the lines," Luke says as we walk toward my house. Or, should I say, he walks and I clomp.

"That's okay," I say, "It's not your fault." Clomp, clomp.

"I think he gets nervous around Lexi since he likes her so much." He reaches up as we pass under a tree and lets his fingers brush the leaves. God, he's tall.

"Jared likes Lexi?" I ask, feigning innocence.

"Oh, yeah, he's totally into her," Luke says. "It seems like she likes Matt, though. I keep telling him he has to stop being a jerk to her, but he just winks and tells me it's part of his master plan." He rolls his eyes.

Great. Not only is Jared telling everyone about his Lexi crush, now Luke is giving Jared love advice. Good love advice. "I think our project is going to be really good," I say. It's lame, but I'm desperate to change the subject. Besides, my head can't take too much more stress. I'm already concentrating on walking without falling and dying. These shoes are seriously dangerous.

"Yeah, it definitely is," Luke says. "So did your mom

calm down a little after I left the other night?"

I giggle. "Yeah. Well, as much as she can, anyway. She was still a little mad at me for getting my hair highlighted, but I got back on her good side by agreeing to babysit for my sister."

"That was nice of you," Luke says.

"Yeah, well, my parents are working on . . ." I try to think of the right word. Their marriage? Their relationship? " . . . stuff, and anything I can do to make it easier for them isn't a big deal to me."

"Yeah, I know what you mean," Luke says. "When my parents got divorced, it was really hard on both of them, but I tried to make sure me and my little brothers stayed out of trouble." He grins. "Although now that things are a little more stable . . ."

I giggle again. The sun is out, and it's casting stripes of light against the sidewalk as we walk.

"I'm glad we got to be partners," Luke says. We pass under a tree and a breeze blows through, and with it comes the scent I'm starting to associate with Luke, a boy smell that I've never noticed on a guy before.

"Definitely," I say. I wonder what sort of torture Kim is going to put me through in order to keep my secret. Maybe she'll make me do all her English homework. Actually, that wouldn't be so bad. I actually like

English. Or maybe she'll make me follow her around and carry her books or something. I rack my brain for all the movies I've seen that have mean girls in them, and try to think of what kind of torture could be in store for me. I'm so caught up in my brain, trying to think about what could happen, that I almost don't realize how close Luke and I are walking to each other. In fact, I don't realize it until he reaches out and takes my hand.

Luke. And. I. Are. Holding. Hands.

And not in a "Let me take your hand and cross the street kind of way." It's definitely in a "We're boyfriend and girlfriend" kind of way. His fingers are intertwined with mine. His hand feels warm. And secure. Not sweaty or weird, the way I sometimes figured it would be to hold hands with a boy.

We don't talk all the way back to my house. It's like the fact that we're now holding hands has compromised our ability to verbalize. This is not how things are supposed to happen. Luke is not supposed to be holding my hand. Jared is supposed to be holding my hand. Or at least pretending to. Does this mean Luke wants to be my boyfriend? And if he does, do I want to be his girlfriend? Do I like Luke? And if I do, what am I supposed to do about my fake boyfriend, Jared? I can't have two boyfriends, even if one is fake.

"Thanks for walking me home," I say when we get in front of my house.

"No problem," he says. He looks at me for a second, and suddenly I think maybe he's going to kiss me. I drop his hand and turn around quickly, trying to look cool, like I have boys holding my hand every day. Then I walk quickly up the driveway and to my front door without looking back. Well, as quickly as I can in these shoes.

That night, while my parents are out, I help Katie make an Olympic podium. We take a bunch of cardboard boxes that we find in the garage and set them up so the biggest one is in the middle. Then we put newspaper down and use some of my mom's craft paint to paint the numbers one, two, and three on them in swirly purple figures.

"Now," Katie says when the paint's dry. "You put my gold medal on me, and give a speech."

"The Olympic Committee is so happy to present you with this gold medal," I say, putting it around her neck. "You deserve it." I grab some fake flowers from the vase on the table and hand them to her.

"Thank you so very much," she says. "I would like to thank my mom, my dad, and my sister, Devon, for making all my dreams come true. This night wouldn't be as special if they weren't all here, supporting me and being proud." I don't think you get to make a speech at the Olympics, but whatever. I reach over and press play on the CD player we've set up to play the national anthem.

Katie puts her hand over her heart and stares solemnly into space. My parents walk in halfway through "The Star-Spangled Banner."

"What in the world—" my mom asks, amused.

"Shh!" Katie shushes her. "No talking during the ceremony."

My parents are silent and put their hands over their hearts until the song is over, and then burst into applause. "Thank you, thank you," Katie says, bowing. Not sure you really do that at the Olympics either, but again, whatever.

"You guys made this?" my dad asks, checking out our podium.

"Yup," I say.

"You did a really great job," he says, sounding surprised.

He and my mom exchange a look.

"Devon, we want you to know how proud of you we are lately," my mom says. "Watching Katie has helped us a lot, and you haven't complained once. We know she gets a little cranky when we leave, but you've been really amazing with handling her."

"Thanks," I say, feeling pleased. But in the back of my mind, I can't help but wonder how proud my parents would be if they knew their oldest daughter was basically lying to everyone but them.

chapter eight

By the time Monday morning rolls around, I have a knot in my stomach the size of the Empire State Building. I spent all weekend dreading going to school, and now that I have to, I feel like I might pass out from stress. Do people even do that? Pass out from stress, I mean. Probably not. I think they just get ulcers.

I avoided everyone for the rest of the weekend, leaving an away message up on my instant messenger and telling my mom that I had so much homework, I couldn't possibly come to the phone. I spent a lot of time in my room, supposedly working on all the homework I allegedly had, but really I was watching TV and reading one of the romance novels I took from my grandma's house this summer. I also spent a lot of time looking at my hand. I know it sounds really weird, but I can't stop thinking about Luke and how it felt to hold his hand, to feel his fingers around mine, to feel the bottom of his shirt brushing against my wrist as we walked.

I head to my locker right off the bus on Monday, my plan being to grab my books and head immediately to homeroom. I'm in such a hurry that my lock doesn't open on the first couple of tries. Crap. 18 right, 27 left, 15 right. I spin right by 15 again, but give it a hopeful yank. I take a deep breath and try again. Yes! The lock springs open, and I reach in and start loading all the books I need for the morning into my bag. Almost done. If I can just get into homeroom before—

"Hey!" a voice chirps right next to my ear. I scream and drop my bag. Books and papers go everywhere.

"Geez," Mel says, kneeling down with me to help me pick up my stuff. "Someone's on a short fuse."

"Thank God it's you," I say, breathing a sigh of relief. "I'm trying to avoid everyone else."

"Everyone else who?" she asks.

"Kim, Lexi, Jared, Luke, everyone," I say. I accidentally step on my math notes, putting a big footprint over a bunch of algebra equations. Great. I hope

I can still read it—we have a test tomorrow.

"Why, what's going on?" Mel asks. She picks up my science homework and puts it back in my purple folder. "I called you three times yesterday. Since when do you have so much homework that you can't come to the phone?" That's the problem with having a best friend. You can never lie to them, because they'll always figure out the truth. I think again about how Mel still doesn't know about my parents, and even more uneasiness passes through me.

"I know," I say. "I'm sorry, it's just that—"

"Uh-oh," Mel says, looking down the hall behind me.

"Uh-oh what?" I ask.

"Hey, Devi," I hear Luke's voice behind me.

"Oh," I say, getting up from the floor. I wipe my hands on my jeans, trying to get some of the grime from the floor off. I glance around quickly to make sure no one else is around. "What's going on?"

"I tried calling you yesterday," he says, "but your mom said you had a ton of homework." My heart is beating erratically in my chest, like when someone has their music up too loud in their car.

"Yeah, I was swamped."

"Cool." He runs his hands through his hair. "I was

afraid you were maybe avoiding me."

"Oh, no, nothing like that." Why, yes, I was avoiding you, Luke, you and pretty much everyone else because I'm a horrible liar who doesn't want to get caught. Mel coughs from the floor, where she's pretending to pick up my papers but is really listening to everything that's going on.

"Good," he says, smiling. He reaches over and takes my hand again. Oh my God. Why does Luke keep holding my hand? And why do I like it so much? Mel coughs again. "I wanted to know if maybe you wanted to hang out after school, maybe get an ice cream or something."

Is Luke asking me out on a date? I can't go out on a date with Luke! Lexi thinks Jared is my boyfriend. How would it look if Luke and I started dating? This is not good. This is bad. This is beyond bad.

"Actually," I say, "I really can't today. I have to take care of my little sister."

"Again?" he asks.

"Yes." I nod. "My parents work a lot, and Katie's only five, so . . ."

"Right." Pause. "How about tomorrow?"

"Babysitting." I swallow.

"Okay, well, maybe another time then."

"Yeah, sure," I say, trying to sound noncommittal. I drop his hand. Holding hands with Luke in public is definitely not a good idea. What if Lexi sees? Or what if someone else sees and tells Lexi? It might be my imagination, but I think I see a look of hurt and confusion pass across Luke's face.

"So I guess I'll catch ya later, then," he says.

"Yeah, definitely. Catch ya later."

"Bye, Melissa," he says to a still-crouched-down Mel.

"Bye," she says, straightening up. "What was that about?" she demands once he's out of earshot.

"What was what about?" I ask.

"You and Luke holding hands." She throws her hands up in exasperation.

"I'm actually not sure what that's about." I have butterflies in my stomach. "He did it the other day too. I'm not sure what it means."

"He did it the other day?" Mel gasps.

"Yeah, he walked me home from Jared's on Saturday."

"And you didn't tell me." She crosses her arms across her chest and raises her eyebrows.

"Well, I haven't talked to you," I say. "So that's why."

"I called you three times yesterday," she repeats.

"Mel . . ."

She glances into my locker, where our BFF notebook is sitting on the top shelf. I haven't even looked at it since the last time she wrote in it. "Did you write me back?"

"Um, no, not yet," I say, pulling down the notebook. "But I'm going to today, I just haven't been—"

"Whatever," she says. She hands me my bag. "Here. I should get to homeroom." She turns around and marches down the hall, leaving me at my locker, staring after her.

I have to break up with him. Or he has to break up with me. Or we have to have a mutual breakup. Everything is getting way too complicated. Jared likes Lexi, Kim knows the truth, Mel is mad at me, and Luke and his hand-holding are about to break the whole story wide open. So at lunch, I corner Lexi and tell her I need to talk to her about something.

"What's up, Devi?" she asks as I drag her into the bathroom.

"Listen, Lexi, something happened and I wanted you to be the first one to know about it," I say. I catch a glimpse of my reflection in the mirror over the sinks and I put on my best serious face. I try to imagine what I would feel like if Jared really *had* broken up with me. I'm shocked to find that now that I know Jared a little better, I don't think I'd be all that upset if he *did* break up with me. Which is going to make this a very challenging acting job.

"Oh my God, Devi, what is it?" Lexi asks, concern on her face.

"Well, the thing is . . ." Lexi looks at me expectantly. "The thing is, Jared and I broke up."

Lexi gasps. Her hand flies to her mouth. "Devi, no! I can't believe it!"

"Me neither," I say. Understatement.

"What happened?"

"I'm not sure," I say slowly. "I mean, we hadn't been getting along, you know that." Lexi nods, but doesn't say anything, which I'm assuming means I'm supposed to continue. "So, uh, this morning before school he IM'd me. And said he didn't want to go out with me anymore."

"He broke up with you over IM?! Devi, that's despicable! To not even have the decency to do it to your face. Or on the phone even." Wow. Lexi's all fired up.

"I know. So that's that," I say. "It's over." Again, understatement.

"Are you okay?" She reaches out and takes my hand. "Do you need anything?"

"No," I say. "Not really." I wonder if I should squeeze out a few tears. I try to think of sad things. Children in third world countries. This movie I saw once where the mother dies. I blink experimentally. Nothing. Hmm. I give a sniff and hope it will suffice.

"He's such a jerk," Lexi says. She squeezes her fists together at her sides. "I always thought you were too good for him."

"You did?" How sweet. I almost forgot how loyal Lexi is. Over the summer, we entered this DDR tournament, and even though this other girl, Sacha Graves, wanted to be Lexi's partner, Lexi stuck with me because she'd already promised. Sacha was the reigning champion, and she and Lexi would have totally won.

"Yes," Lexi says, nodding. She's wearing dangly red heart earrings that jangle as she moves her head. "He's such a jerk, and you're such a nice person, Devi. Like how you made me feel welcome here when I was new."

I did? "I did?" For some reason, this, coupled with thinking about Lexi being my partner in the DDR tournament, makes me feel horrible. I'm a fraud. And a bad friend.

"Of course!" Lexi nods up and down. "You let me hang with you and your friends. And Jared is just so . . ." She makes a face. "He's cute and everything, Devi, but really. You can do so much better." I relax slightly. If Lexi doesn't like Jared, then I'm not keeping them apart. Of course, if he weren't being such a jerk to her, maybe she *would* like him. She turns around and faces the mirror and reaches up to smooth her hair.

"Devi, do you think I should get my hair highlighted like yours?" She pulls a strand down and studies it critically.

"Definitely," I say. "Then we could be twins."

"Fab!" She turns around and gives me a huge smile. Her braces sparkle. "You ready to go back?"

"Actually, um, I think I'm going to go to the library for lunch. I just think it would be weird seeing Jared right now." Actually, I want to go to the library because Mel's there, and I feel horrible about the way we left things this morning.

"I understand," Lexi says. "I'll look for you after school." She blows me a kiss. When she's gone, I wash my hands and then take a brush out of my bag and run it through my hair. I take a deep breath. Everything's fine. Mel will forgive me, I'll be able to hang out with Luke, Kim won't have anything on me, and Jared will never find out that I told anyone we were together. Everything can finally go back to being normal. I shove my brush back in my bag. Twenty minutes left of lunch. More than enough time to get back on Mel's good side.

Suddenly the door to the bathroom opens and Kim storms in.

"Devi," she says. The door slams against the wall from the force of her pushing it open. Wow. Kim's really strong for someone who is so small.

"Hi," I say. "Listen, I just told Lexi that Jared and I broke up, so—"

"No, you listen," she says, cutting me off. For a second, I'm afraid she's going to hit me or something. Am I going to get in a fistfight? "I know Luke likes you. And if you go out with him, if you even *think* about starting to hang out with him, I'll tell everyone you lied."

"I need to talk to you," I say, setting my books down on the library table across from Mel.

"I can't really talk right now, Devon," she says, not looking up. She's bent over her math book, her hair brushing against the table. Her pencil makes scraping sounds as it moves quickly across her paper.

"Please," I say, "I'm begging you." She keeps writing and doesn't look up. "Okay, look," I say, sliding into the seat across from her. "I know I haven't been the best friend lately. I'm sorry. And you've been nothing but great to me, and doing what you did, pretending to like Jared when you really think he's horrible . . ." I swallow around the lump in my throat. "But Mel, I really, really, need you right now. And I don't know who else to talk to."

She sighs and sets her pencil down. "I only have a second."

I nod seriously. I fill her in quickly on what's been going on, how I fed Lexi the fake breakup story and how everything ended in the bathroom with Kim threatening my life. Okay, so she didn't threaten my life, exactly, but close enough.

"I don't understand why she would do that," I say. "Why would Kim not want me to like Luke? Does she hate me that much? Is she that determined to keep me out of her group? She hardly even knows me."

Mel sighs and looks at me like I'm an idiot. "Devon, did you ever stop to think that maybe Kim likes Luke?"

Oh. Right. I did kind of suspect that. "But if she likes him, then why doesn't she just ask him out? She could have any guy she wanted."

"Maybe he doesn't like her," Mel says, shrugging. "Maybe she's already tried to get him to go out with her and he said no."

"I should pump Lexi to see if she knows anything," I say, glancing at the clock and wondering if it's too late to find her again before lunch ends.

Mel pulls a Baggie of trail mix out of her backpack and takes a handful, munches on it thoughtfully, and then holds it out to me. "Thanks," I say. With all this drama, I've completely forgotten to eat lunch.

"You know," Mel says, glancing at me out of the corner of her eye. "The other thing you could do is just tell the truth."

Gasp. "No way." Is Mel crazy? "You know that if I do that, I'll be a social outcast."

"Maybe, maybe not," she says. "At least you could relax a little bit."

"I'll think about it," I lie. Ten minutes left in lunch, which means if I sprint back to the cafeteria I can be there in two minutes, one minute to find Lexi, one minute to get her away from everyone else, and six minutes to pump her for info about Kim and Luke. "Listen, I'm going to head back to the caf. Call me later and we'll make a plan to hang out. I promise." I grab another handful of trail mix and run back to the cafeteria.

"Lexi," I say, approaching the A-list table. Kim looks up and glares at me. "Can I talk to you for a second?"

"Of course!" she says. She has a sympathetic look on her face, probably because she thinks it's about Jared dumping me. I wonder if I should have spun the story the other way, that I dumped Jared. How cool would that be, me dumping the hottest guy in school? Of course, it was a fictitious relationship, which means it would have been a fictitious breakup, but still. "Are you okay?" Lexi asks, once we're out of earshot. She strokes my arm and looks at me seriously.

"Yes," I say. Lexi looks surprised. "I mean, I'm okay. I will be okay, anyway." I lean closer to her so that there's no chance anyone will overhear us. "So listen, I was wondering, um, do you know if Kim likes Luke?"

"I don't know," Lexi says, shrugging. "I don't think so."

"Oh, okay." Relief floods my body. If Kim liked Luke, Lexi would know about it, right? I mean, they're friends.

"Why?" Lexi asks. "Do you like Luke?" She looks at me excitedly. "Maybe you should just ask her."

"Uh, I don't know if I like him. I'm definitely not going to go after him," I say, hoping by telling Lexi it will get back to Kim. "I don't know if I'm ready to start liking someone else."

Lexi pats me again. "I totally understand." Matt O'Connor comes up behind Lexi and pulls her hair. She squeals in delight and turns around. "Matt, stop!" she says, but you can tell she's totally loving it. He grins at her and heads toward the lunch table.

"What's going on with you two?" I ask.

"I dunno," she says, flushing. "We went to play DDR this weekend, and it was really fun. He wouldn't let me pay for any games, and he kept trying to win me stuffed animals."

Lexi still has her head turned, watching Matt walk through the lunchtime crowd to our table. She turns back to me. "Devi, I'm so sorry, here I am going on and on about Matt and how cool he is, and you're totally having a romantic crisis." She squeezes my arm. "So do you want me to ask Kim if she likes Luke?" she asks. She twirls a strand of her hair around her finger and looks at it critically. "I totally need a haircut. I'm definitely going to get mine like yours."

"Yeah, that would be cool," I say. "You talking to Kim, I mean. And getting your hair like mine too." I nod. "Just make sure that Kim doesn't know you're asking for me."

"Of course, Devi," Lexi says, nodding seriously. "You can trust me." I don't point out that the last time she promised I could trust her, she ended up leaking the secret. Of course, that was a made-up secret, but still.

"Great."

"Devi, can I talk to you for a second?" Jared asks, walking up to us.

"No, you cannot," Lexi says, putting her arm around me. "She doesn't want to talk to you." She glares at him. Jared looks confused.

"It's okay, Lexi," I say, detangling myself from her grasp. "I'll be okay."

"Are you sure?"

"Yes," I say, trying to sound forceful.

She heads back to the lunch table, but not before she throws Jared a mean look over her shoulder.

"Dude, that girl is seriously hostile," he says, shaking his head.

"So what's up?" I ask, giving him my brightest

smile. I wonder what Jared would think if he knew he'd just broken up with me.

"I just wanted to talk to you about this Lexi thing."

"Yes?"

"The thing is, I think she likes Matt."

"Why do you think that?" I ask, frowning.

"Because they're always flirting and talking," Jared says. "And they went to the mall together this weekend, alone. And Matt said, 'I like Lexi, and I'm pretty sure she likes me.'"

"I don't know if that's quite true," I say, looking over Jared's shoulder to where Lexi is sitting next to Matt. She takes the hat he's wearing off his head and puts it on her own. Matt starts tickling her, and she giggles.

"Yeah, well, that's what it seems like. So I think maybe I should just tell her I like her."

"No!" I practically scream. Oh, God. Can this day get any more complicated? How is it that one lie has spiraled out of control into all these little subplots? Is it like quantum physics or something? If you lie once, it will reverberate through your universe, screwing everything else up?

"Why not?" Jared asks, frowning. "I don't want her

to start going out with Matt. And being mean to her obviously isn't working. She acts like she hates me."

"She doesn't hate you," I say. "Listen, um, just give it some time."

He looks at me skeptically. "Why?"

"I mean, um, give me some time. To talk to her. I'll find out what's going on between her and Matt, and I'll ask her what she thinks about you."

"You will?" Jared beams. "Thanks, Devi." I'm starting to worry a little bit about Jared's mental state. Being mean to Lexi is obviously not working, and yet even though I'm the one who gave him that obviously horrible advice, he's willing to trust me again.

"No prob," I say, grinning back shakily. Now what?

That night, in an effort to distract myself from the impending doom that is my life, I let Katie convince me to watch *The Cutting Edge* with her. Not that I really have a choice. My parents are seeing their counselor, so I'm stuck babysitting. As Olympics movies go, *The Cutting Edge* is one of my favorites. Skating, cute costumes, romance, and drama. Plus the whole overcoming obstacles to achieve your dreams thing. I mean, what's not to like?

"This is gonna be so fun, right, Devon?" Katie asks. She pulls the DVD out of its case and throws the case on the floor.

"Right," I say, not really meaning it. The problem with watching a movie with Katie is that since she watches her DVDs over and over, she usually has the movie memorized. And she quotes it. Like, actually says the lines along with the actors as they're saying them. Which is really annoying.

"Fun, fun, fun," Katie sings, dancing over to the DVD player and popping in the disc. "Say it, Devon," she instructs. "Fun, fun, fun."

"Fun, fun, fun," I recite, resisting the urge to roll my eyes. I'm sprawled on the floor wearing my favorite pair of pajama pants (they're pink and say SLEEPYTIME on the butt—they're my favorite because my mom bought them for me right before I went to stay with my grandma for the summer, and even though they were new, for some reason they smelled like her, so I wore them every night), and a big T-shirt of my dad's that says CORNELL on it. I have my math book open in front of me because I have a ton of homework, but I plan on using it as an excuse for why I'm not paying exact attention to the movie.

"You didn't say it right," Katie admonishes. She grabs the DVD remote and settles into the couch. "And don't pretend you're doing your homework so you don't have to watch the movie. It is a very good flick." She expertly scrolls through the title menu. "And after this movie is over, we will watch it with the director's commentary."

Great.

The opening sequence starts.

"When I become an ice skater I'm going to have a pink costume, very flowing, with no sequins," she says. "I watched them make one just like it on *Project Runway*." She frowns. "But I forget the name of the person who made it." She looks upset for a second, but then shakes her head. "But by then, I'll be famous, so it won't matter, I can find out."

The doorbell rings, saving me from having to hear more.

I scramble up from the floor. "Devon!" Katie screams. "You know we're not supposed to answer the door when Mom and Dad aren't home!"

"I'm not," I say. "I'm just going to look out the peephole." Not like it would matter. With the way Katie just screamed, anyone who's at the door definitely knows someone's home and that whoever it is isn't supposed to answer the door when their parents aren't home.

I step up on my toes in the front hallway and look out the peephole. Oh my God. It's Luke.

"Ohmigod," I say. "It's Luke." Why is Luke here? And who does that? Just shows up at someone's house like this? Without calling or anything?

"Oh," Katie says, looking annoyed. "Just your boyfriend. Don't answer it, we're watching a movie."

"Um, I have to," I say. Katie starts to protest, so I rush on. "It's about school." I put my hands on her shoulders and steer her back toward the living room. "Now go watch the movie and I'll be back in a second."

She stomps off.

"Luke!" I say, opening the door. "What are you doing here?"

"I was hanging out with Jared for a while and I just thought I'd stop by and drop this off." He holds up a piece of paper with drawings on it. "It's a scene-by-scene drawing of our project. Kind of like a storyboard."

"Luke, that's amazing!" I exclaim, looking at the paper. He has little drawings of all of us, saying our lines, and what should happen from scene to scene, complete with camera angles.

"Yeah, well, Matt gave me the idea, and I had some

time in study hall." He shrugs, and I think I see him blush. Is Luke blushing? Did I make Luke blush? How cute! He runs his fingers through his hair and looks at the ground.

"Do you want to come in for a little while?" I ask before thinking. "So we can work on the project," I add quickly. Even though there's really nothing left to do on the project. Except film it, which we're not doing until the weekend.

"Sure," Luke says, moving past me and into the hallway. He's wearing a puffy dark green vest over a long-sleeved T-shirt and a pair of baggy jeans. The sleeve of his shirt brushes against my bare arm as he moves by, and I'm reminded of the time he held my hand. I'm also reminded that I'm wearing a pair of pants that say SLEEPYTIME on the butt, and an old T-shirt. Great.

"Um, I actually just got out of the shower," I lie. "And I was about to get dressed."

He frowns. "You were about to get dressed?" He checks his watch. "It's almost eight o'clock."

"I know, but I don't like to lounge around too much in my pajamas. It makes me unproductive." He looks at me skeptically. "And," I rush on, just in case he's wondering, "my hair isn't wet because I just dried it."

"Okay." He thinks I'm a freak.

"So you wait here," I say, "and I'll run upstairs and get dressed."

"Okay," he says again, sounding doubtful.

I race up the stairs to my room, stubbing my toe on my doorframe in the process. A searing pain shoots from my toe all the way up my leg. Ow. I pick up a pair of jeans off my floor and slide them on. I hope Luke doesn't realize that these are the same pants I wore to school today. He might think I'm a slob if I'm putting dirty clothes on right after I just got out of the shower. I pull my new pink-and-maroon striped sweater out of my closet and slide it on, then smear some lip gloss onto my lips.

I hobble back downstairs, but when I get to the hallway, Luke's not there. I find him in the living room, sitting next to Katie on the couch.

"Do you think they're going to fall in love or not?" Katie asks him.

"Who?" Luke asks.

"Those two!" Katie says, pointing at the TV and looking exasperated. "Even though they hate each other now, do you think they're going to fall in love or not?"

"Hello!" I say brightly.

"Devon, you left Luke standing in the hallway. That wasn't very nice," Katie says. "And why are you limping?"

"I'm not," I say, limping over to the chair in the corner and plopping myself into it. My toe is killing me.

"Let me check," Katie says, hopping off the couch. "Let me check your legs!"

"No, I'm fine," I say. Luke smiles uncomfortably.

"Katie, Luke and I are going to go work in the kitchen," I say, figuring it's better to get away from her than it is to stay in here, where she's obviously feels it's appropriate to act like the ultimate embarrassment. "You stay in here and watch the movie."

I hobble into the kitchen. Luke follows me. I wonder if my toe is broken. That would be horrible. Although maybe they'd give me crutches and everyone would feel sorry for me and I'd get to leave class five minutes early in order to get to my next one on time.

"So," I say, not sure what's supposed to happen now. "Do you want something to drink?"

"Sure," he says. I pull the grape juice out of the refrigerator and take two glasses down from the cupboard. My toe is throbbing. I never realized how many steps it takes to get around the kitchen. I wonder if

Luke would notice if I started hopping on one foot.

"Here you go," I say, sitting his glass down in front of him.

"Thanks." He takes a sip of his juice, and then sits the glass down on the table. He licks a stray drop of juice off his lips, then starts pulling his puffy vest off. Luke is practically undressing at my kitchen table. I take another sip of my drink and try not to stare. In the living room, I can hear Katie reciting the lines to *The Cutting Edge* along with the actors.

"Listen, Devon, I didn't come here to talk about the project."

"Oh," I say, acting cool.

"The other day, when I asked you to hang out, I just . . . I wanted to know if you said no because you really had to babysit, or if you said no because you just didn't want to hang out." He rushes on. "I'm cool either way, I just kind of need to know."

"Why?" I ask, stalling.

"Because if it was really because you just had to babysit, I'm going to ask you out again." He smiles.

"Oh." I quickly run through the options in my mind. I really do like Luke. But if I go out with him, Kim's going to tell everyone that I made up the fact that Jared is my boyfriend. And then it's not going to matter if I'm going out with Luke, because he'll dump me, anyway.

The phone rings then, saving me from having to come up with an answer. I leap to the phone in the kitchen, hoping it's one of those survey people who makes you answer three million questions about what radio station you listen to or what kind of cereal you eat.

"Hello?" I say, trying to sound friendly and like the type of person who has unlimited amounts of time to spend on the phone, answering questions for strangers.

"Hey." It's Mel.

"Hi, Mel," I say. "What's up?"

"Working on the math homework. What are you doing?"

"Um, nothing really. Having some grape juice. Luke's over."

"Luke's there?" she asks, sounding confused. "I thought you had to babysit Katie tonight."

"I did have to babysit Katie," I say. "I mean, I do have to babysit her. I AM babysitting her." I wonder if my sprained toe is somehow compromising my ability to talk. "But Luke's here. We're having grape juice." We're having grape juice? I did not just say that. Luke holds up his glass and smiles uncertainly. Maybe this thing with Luke will just resolve itself. I mean, obviously he won't want to date a crazy person.

"But you have a friend over," Mel says, sounding almost mad.

"It was kind of unexpected."

"Fine," Mel says. "Call me when you're done dealing with things that are unexpected." And then she hangs up on me. I stare at the receiver in shock. Mel has never hung up on me, ever. In fact, if you asked me, "Who is the person least likely to ever hang up on you?", I would have answered Mel.

"She hung up on me," I say to no one in particular, still looking at the receiver.

"Is she mad at you?" Luke asks.

"Apparently." I replace the phone back on the cradle and sit back down in my chair. I feel dazed.

"How come?"

"I'm not sure," I say. "I guess it's because we haven't been spending all that much time together lately. I've just been busy with Lexi and . . . other things." Other things = my fake boyfriend and Kim trying to ruin my life.

"That must be hard for her," Luke says. He picks up his grape juice and drains the rest of it. "You hanging out with all these new friends."

"But I've tried to include her in everything I'm doing," I say. "I always invite her anywhere I go." But as I'm saying it, I realize it isn't exactly true. Sure, I invited Mel to sit with us at lunch, but that was more for my own security. And I pretty much told her she couldn't come to Jared's house to work on the project. And then there was the time I went to the mall with Kim and Lexi . . .

"It's still probably hard for her," Luke says. "To have to share you. She's probably used to it being just the two of you. Plus weren't you away all summer? She probably just misses her friend."

"Yeah," I say, feeling a lump rise in my throat. Spraining my toe is probably the universe's way of punishing me for being such a terrible person. It would serve me right if I got a disgusting toe fungus that spread from my toe to my entire body and killed me. And then of course no one would come to my funeral since I'm such a horrible friend. I feel my eyes start to water.

"Oh, hey," Luke says, "don't cry."

"I'm not," I say, wiping my eyes with the sleeve of my sweater. He gets up from the other side of the table and comes over and sits in the chair next to me. He takes my hand.

"Look, I'm sure you can work it out, whatever it

is. Haven't you guys been friends since, like, second grade?"

"Yes," I say, which makes me feel like I want to cry even more. How could I have let something so stupid get in the way of a friendship I've had since second grade?

"So you guys will be fine," he says. His finger is making little circles on my palm. "You just have to let her cool off a little bit, and then have a talk with her. Let her know you still care. Maybe do something nice for her?"

"You think?" I ask, trying not to sniff.

"Definitely."

"Maybe you're right," I say, trying to think of something nice I can do for Mel. Sometimes people at school decorate each other's lockers for their birthdays, or if someone has a big game or something. Maybe I could decorate her locker tomorrow for no reason. Just as a BFF kind of thing, to let her know that I care.

"Thanks," I say.

"No problem," Luke says. We sit there for a second, not saying anything, just holding hands.

The phone rings again, breaking the spell, and I leap up from my chair.

"No, Lexi," I hear Katie saying from the cordless phone in the living room. "Devon can't talk right now because she's in the kitchen with her boyfriend."

Oh, God. "Katie, I got it," I say. "Hang up."

"Okaaay," Katie sings. The phone clicks off.

"Devi!" Lexi says. "What are you doing? And who's over? Did you and Jared make up?"

"Me and Jared?" I ask before I realize that Luke can hear. I glance over to the table, but he doesn't appear to have noticed. Or if he did, he hasn't reacted.

"Yes!" Lexi says. "Katie said your boyfriend was over."

"Is it okay if I grab some more juice?" Luke asks, standing up and heading to the refrigerator.

"Yes, that's fine," I say.

"Ohmigod, is that Luke?" Lexi practically screams in my ear. "Devi, what is going on, are you two going out now?"

"No," I say. "No, um, we're working on our project." Luke pours some more juice into his glass, and then fills mine as well. How sweet.

"Oh," Lexi says, sounding disappointed. "Well, don't feel bad."

"Um, don't feel bad about what?" I ask. This is getting stressful, the phone always ringing when Luke is sitting in my kitchen.

"That your love life isn't going that well." Lexi sighs. "Mine isn't going so well either."

"Uh, it isn't?"

"No," she says, "It isn't. I hung out with Matt tonight. We went to play DDR again at the mall, and I thought we had a good time, but he said he'd IM me later and he hasn't."

"That sucks," I say, glancing over to the table where Luke is looking at the paper on which he sketched out our skit. He's bent over the storyboard, looking at it intently. I can't believe I never realized how hot he is. Much hotter than Jared. And much smarter, too. And nicer. And I bet he doesn't have *Star Wars* book covers, either.

"Hello!" Lexi's saying. "So what should I do?"

"Um, well, does he have an away message up?"

"Are you even listening to me?" Lexi asks, exasperated. "He doesn't have an away message up! And I've IM'd him six times and he hasn't replied."

Six times? Yikes. "Wow."

"I know! It makes no sense whatsoever. Listen, do you want to go to the mall tomorrow? I want to get my hair done, and we can talk about this more."

There's a click on the line, and Lexi's mom's voice

comes over the phone from another extension. "Lexi? Are you on the phone?"

"Yes," Lexi says, sighing.

"Well, please get off. I have to schedule a tanning appointment, and the salon is about to close." She clicks off.

"Ugh," Lexi says. "Anyway, so do you want to go tomorrow?"

"Sure," I say. "Oh, and, um, before you go, have you had a chance to talk to Kim yet?"

"No," Lexi says. "but I'll try to IM her tonight, since she's obviously the only one I'll be talking to on instant messenger." Such a drama queen, that Lexi.

"Okay, thanks," I say. I hang up the phone. And when I turn around, my mom's standing in the kitchen, her hands on her hips. She's looking from me to Luke and she doesn't look happy.

chapter nine

"Nothing is going on!" I say. **"Mom, you** are freaking out over nothing."

My mom is not taking the whole Luke-being-over-while-I-was-babysitting-Katie thing that well. In fact, she's freaking out. After she sent Luke home (which was quite embarrassing because she was perfectly nice about it, but you could tell she was really upset, which almost made it worse, because it was pretty obvious that as soon as he left she was going to yell at me), she sat me down in the living room, sent Katie to bed, and sent my dad upstairs to their bedroom. She sent Katie away because she wanted to talk to me alone, and she sent my dad upstairs because she saw on *Dr. Phil* that the relationship you have with the parent of your same sex is the most important, and that sometimes while dealing with sensitive issues, it's important for a mom to talk to her daughter alone.

"Devon, you know the rules," my mom says. She runs her hand through her curly hair. "You are not to have anyone in the house while your father and I are gone. You're not to answer the door, you're not to tell anyone you're home alone, and you are certainly not supposed to have BOYS OVER."

"Mom, I know," I say. "But we were working on our project, and I didn't think you'd mind."

"You should have called my cell phone to check." I actually had thought of that. Calling her cell phone, I mean. But I figured she'd say no.

"I was going to," I say, "but then I hurt my toe while I was going upstairs and I forgot about it." I hold my toe up to show her, but she's not having it.

"Devon, it's important that your father and I are able to trust you while we're not here."

"Mom, I know," I say. "You can trust me. But, really, there's nothing going on with me and Luke. I promise." She narrows her eyes and looks at me doubtfully. I can't believe this. My mom thinks I invited Luke over here so that we could make out while she wasn't home. How is it that it's so easy for my mom to think I have a boyfriend, yet it's taking so much effort and confusion to make other people believe I have a *fake* boyfriend? "Didn't you just say the other night what a great job I was doing?"

"That doesn't change the fact that you shouldn't have had a friend over while your father and I weren't home."

"You're right," I say, nodding. "You're absolutely right. Which is why it's never going to happen again. And I'm sorry I broke your trust." Dr. Phil says teens need to take responsibility for their actions and apologize for what they did wrong. Parents are not the enemy.

"Devon, it's not that easy," my mom says. I'm not sure if setting boundaries is good for our parent-child relationship. Especially since it leads to me getting in trouble for things I didn't even do. Besides, this summer, when my mom was all about being boundary-less, my life was way less complicated, and I had way cuter shoes. "You're going to have to be punished for this."

"Mom! Please, that is so unfair!" This is ridiculous. How can she possibly punish me for doing absolutely nothing? "We were working on schoolwork!"

"I don't care," she says, standing up from the couch.

She crosses her arms and paces back and forth in front of me. "And if you were just doing schoolwork, then why didn't you ask me beforehand?"

"Because he just showed up here," I say. "You can ask Katie. I had no idea he was coming over."

She looks at what I'm wearing. "You're awfully dressed up for someone who wasn't expecting company." I put my hand on my lips self-consciously. I can still feel some of the lip gloss I smeared on when Luke first got here.

"Mom, I changed when he got here."

"But you guys were just doing schoolwork, and there's nothing going on between the two of you?"

I can feel myself starting to get upset, and my chest starts to get tight. "Devon, you're grounded from the phone, your computer, and going out for two weeks."

I start to protest, but she holds up her hand. "You can go to Jared's this weekend to work on your project, but that's it. You'll come straight home."

"Mom, you're being really unfair," I say, trying to keep my voice calm even though I feel like I'm going to cry.

"I'm not changing my mind," she says.

"Fine." I get up from the couch and walk haughtily

up the stairs. Well, as haughtily as I can with my bad toe, which feels much better but is still kind of hurting. I yank my clothes off and throw them into a pile in the floor, then pull my SLEEPYTIME pajama pants and COR-NELL T-shirt back on. I flip my light switch and climb into bed, not even bothering to wash my face or brush my teeth. I feel the tears start to slip down my face, and I don't fall asleep for a long time.

The next morning, I'm waiting for Mel at her locker with a sign that says HAPPY BFF DAY! Get it? It's kind of like Happy Birthday, only it's Happy BFF day. It's kind of corny, but whatever. I got to school an hour early and used the glitter and stuff in the art room to make a bunch of signs, and I blew up some balloons we had leftover from Katie's birthday party last month. But Mel never shows up, and finally I have to head off to homeroom.

By lunchtime, Mel is still nowhere to be found. She's not in school, which makes me worried. Matt, however, *is* in school, and seems to be blowing Lexi off. They don't talk all through lunch, and Matt ignores Lexi to flirt with Kayleigh Trusco, who wears a C-cup bra.

When Lexi's mom drops us off at the mall that

afternoon, neither one of us is in a great mood.

"I just don't understand it," Lexi says, flipping through a rack of long, striped sweaters at bebe. "He kept telling me how cool I was, and how much he liked me." She looks at me out of the corner of her eye. "Devi, can you keep a secret?" Oh, God. The word "secret" makes the hairs on the back of my neck stand up. But I nod.

"He kissed me," she whispers. "After school, by the buses the other day. He just leaned in and kissed me." She brushes her fingers against her lips like she can't quite believe it happened, or is trying to remember exactly what it felt like.

"Wow," I say, trying to relate. Which is hard, because I've never been kissed.

"He's a good kisser," she says. She starts moving the sweaters on the rack faster. Fabric goes flying by in a sea of blues, pinks, and purples, faster and faster as Lexi pushes them. "Was Jared a good kisser?"

"Was Jared a good kisser?" I repeat, trying to stall for time. "Um, yes. A very good kisser."

"Oh, Devi, I'm so sorry," she says, squeezing my hand. "Guys are such jerks." She pulls two sweaters off the rack, a pink and a purple. "We are buying these," she says. "To make ourselves feel better. These are our

'We're going to find better guys' sweaters." I look at her doubtfully. I don't know if I believe a sweater can actually make you feel better. Especially since I'm not all that upset to begin with. Actually, that's not true. I am upset, just not for the reasons Lexi thinks. She thinks I'm upset because Jared dumped me, when in actuality, I'm upset for a myriad of other reasons, including but not limited to the fact that I like a boy I can't have, I'm grounded, my best friend hates me, and somehow I'm only thirteen and living a lie.

"I don't know if a sweater is going to make us feel better," I say, fingering the price tag.

"It's on sale," Devi says. "And we're getting them." She glances around and pulls two shiny silver belts off the rack next to us. "And these to go with them."

"Okay," I say, shrugging. There goes the babysitting money I made last night. But who cares, really? The only reason I'm even here right now is because I lied to my mom about having to stay after school to make up a test. After this, I won't be allowed out of the house for two weeks, so unless I want to spend my money on ordering pizza or bribing Katie to be my slave, I might as well spend it.

"Off to the salon!" Lexi squeals as we walk out of the store, swinging our new purchases.

"Hey, Lexi," I ask, "did you have a chance to talk to Kim at all?"

"Yes," Lexi says, nodding. She maneuvers around some other shoppers, a guy with a pierced eyebrow who walks right between us without even apologizing. "Hello, rude," Lexi mutters.

"And what did she say?" I try to sound nonchalant.

"Yes, she likes him." Lexi says. "She asked him out once, but I guess he wasn't interested, and it's been this whole unrequited love thing for months. Actually, Devi, I'm surprised you didn't know that. Supposedly it's, like, public knowledge."

"Really?" I ask.

"Yeah. Even Jared knew, and he seems totally clueless." My heart suddenly drops into my stomach.

"When did you talk to Jared?"

"Today for a little while. He came into my study hall to make up a test, and I was asking him about Matt. He was actually being sweet to me for once." Great. So much for Jared ignoring Lexi and blowing her off. That boy refuses to listen to me. Which I guess actually makes him smarter than I give him credit for.

Lexi and I walk into the hair salon, and the smell of chemicals and shampoo hits my nose. I inhale.

I'm actually starting to like the smell of hair salons. It reminds me of being pretty, of getting ready to go places.

"I have an appointment at four," Lexi tells the receptionist, who starts flipping through the appointment book in front of her.

"It'll be just a second," she says.

Lexi turns to me. "Anyway, Jared says not to worry about Matt, that that's kind of what he does with girls." She pulls a mirror out of her purse and starts smoothing her hair. Which makes no sense, since she's about to get it done. Why would she be fixing her hair before she's about to get it cut? Isn't that like trying to feel better before you go to the doctor's? And isn't it easier for them to work on your hair if it's a big mess? I mean, they're going to wash it for her. That's why there's all those horrible shots of celebrities in those celeb magazines—the paparazzi catch them when they're looking horrible and on their way to the salon.

"What do you mean?" I ask, not sure I'm liking the fact that Jared and Lexi talked for so long. What's up with that? And how could he have been talking to her while he was supposed to be making up a test?

"He said Matt is a great friend, but that he tends to move from girl to girl." She snaps her compact shut and slides it back into her purse. "And he told me not to feel bad."

"I think he's right," I say. "You shouldn't worry about it. You're way too good for that."

I spend the next hour leafing through *Seventeen* magazine while Lexi gets her hair done. It takes longer than I thought, and I'm starting to get a little anxious. There's no way my mom's going to believe that it took this long to make up a test. Maybe I can tell her it was a really long test. With lots of essays.

When Lexi finally emerges from the chair, she does a little twirl. "We're twins!" she says, smiling. Lexi and I now have the same haircut and highlights.

"Great!" I say brightly, hustling Lexi out of the salon. "Now let's call your mom so she can come get us."

"Don't you want to shop some more?" Lexi stops in front of a store to admire her reflection in the windows. "I need to show off my new haircut." She pouts her lips at herself and then smiles.

"I'd like to," I say. "But technically I'm grounded, remember?"

"Oh." She looks disappointed. "Right."

"So come on," I say, walking quickly toward the other side of the mall, where Lexi's mom always picks us up. "Let's go." I wonder how I'm going to sneak my sweater into the house. Put it in my backpack, I guess. I'm so preoccupied with making sure I don't get caught that it takes me a second to realize that Lexi is no longer walking with me. I turn around, and she's a few feet behind, stopped in her tracks.

"Come on," I say. What is the deal? I thought Lexi had mentioned something about running track at her old school. She'll never make the team here if that's her normal pace. "What are you looking at?" Lexi's staring straight ahead, and when I follow her gaze, I realize why she stopped. Because coming up the escalator is Matt O'Connor. And he's holding Kim's hand.

"I can't believe she would do that!" Lexi rages. We're in Lexi's mom's car on the way home, and although Lexi was quiet while we waited outside the mall for our ride, once she buckled her seat belt, she started becoming more vocal.

"So this was your boyfriend?" Lexi's mom asks, sounding confused. She slows down at a yellow light. I'm never going to get home on time if Lexi's mom keeps driving like this. She's about as fast as a dial-up connection.

"Not exactly," Lexi says. "But we were moving in that direction. He kissed me by the buses."

Mrs. Cortland nods, and once again I marvel at how different she is from my own mom. Lexi basically tells her she was making out with a guy who wasn't even her boyfriend and her mom accepts this as being normal. I'm working on a project with a boy in my own home, with my little sister two feet away, and my mom acts like I'm two steps away from becoming a teen parent. "Well," Lexi's mom says, "it sounds like you need to win him back."

"Win him back?" Lexi asks, frowning.

"Yes," Mrs. Cortland says. "You have a new haircut now, which is a great first step." She looks at the bag from bebe that's on the front seat next to Lexi. "And you bought new clothes?"

"Yeah," Lexi says. "Devi and I bought matching sweaters."

Mrs. Cortland frowns again, but recovers quickly. "You can get him back, Lexi. You're beautiful."

"I don't know, Mom," Lexi says, looking doubtful. "It's not that easy."

"Of course it is," Mrs. Cortland persists.

"He kind of moves from girl to girl," Lexi explains.

"Did Kim know that you like him?" Mrs. Cortland asks, ignoring Lexi's last remark. The light turns green, and she takes her time before pushing the gas pedal and going through it. I squirm in the backseat.

"Of course she knew!" Lexi says. "Everyone knew!" They did?

"She sounds like she's not a very nice friend," Lexi's mom says.

"She definitely isn't," Lexi says.

"Hey," I say. "I thought Kim liked Luke, anyway. What's she doing going after Matt?"

"I should have known it was coming," Lexi moans. "Jared said Kim only goes after guys she thinks other people like. It's like she has to prove that she's better than them."

"So she only went after Luke because she thought he liked me?"

"Jared says that's what she does!" Lexi throws her hands up in the air. "It's so diabolical." She turns around and looks at me. "That's the word Jared used to describe it. Diabolical. And you know that it must be true if Jared is calling her that. Since they're friends and all."

Apparently Lexi and Jared had quite the chat, complete with big words and everything. This is troubling, but I don't have too much time to dwell on it, because Mrs. Cortland is pulling into my driveway. I quickly unzip my backpack and shove the bag from bebe into it. Lexi's mom is watching me in the rearview mirror. She probably thinks I stole it.

"Your parents are home, right, Devon?" she asks. Her brows knit in concern. I resist the urge to roll my eyes.

"My mom's home, yeah," I say. "I'll see you in school tomorrow, Lexi." I reach over the seat and squeeze her shoulder reassuringly. "And we'll figure out what to do about this."

"Bye," Lexi says forlornly. "Don't forget to wear your sweater and belt tomorrow."

I jump out of the car and race toward the house. I'm half-expecting my mom to be waiting at the door, her hands on her hips and some kind of note in her hand from the school that says: DEVON DID NOT HAVE TO STAY AFTER TODAY. IF SHE TOLD YOU THAT SHE DID, IT'S BECAUSE SHE WAS LYING SO SHE COULD GO SHOPPING AT THE MALL WITH LEXI CORTLAND.

But when I get in the house, my mom's at the kitchen table, working on her laptop, and all she says is, "Hi, honey. How did your test go?"

I collapse into the kitchen chair. "Fine," I say. But later, as I'm taking my new clothes out of my bookbag, I don't feel fine at all.

chapter ten

The next morning before homeroom, I wait for Mel at her locker again. I have no idea why she wasn't in school yesterday. I couldn't call her last night because I'm grounded from the phone, and I couldn't IM her because I'm grounded from the computer.

When I see her coming down the hall, her blue backpack bouncing on her shoulder, I feel an immediate sense of relief.

"Hey," she says when she sees me.

"Hey," I say, not sure how I'm supposed to act. I mean, the last time we talked, Mel hung up on me.

"Are you still mad at me?" I ask her.

"That depends on what you mean by mad," she says. She twirls the dial on her locker and starts exchanging the books in her bag for the ones she needs for her morning classes.

"By mad, I mean are you speaking to me, are you upset with me, are you going to ignore me?"

"I'm obviously speaking to you. We're speaking right now." She continues taking out her books and doesn't look at me.

"Okaaay," I say. "Um, here's the notebook back." I hold our notebook out to her. I spent all last night writing in it, a long note about how much I missed her, and how even though I knew we hadn't been hanging out much lately, she was still my best friend. She takes the notebook and drops it into her bag wordlessly. Okaaay. "So, um, where were you yesterday?" I try.

"Like you care," she snorts.

"I do!" I say. "I waited for you all morning. I had this whole thing planned with balloons and everything." She looks at me skeptically. Crap. I should have done the BFF locker today, but I wasn't sure if Mel was going to be in school. And yesterday it was a big pain because I had to lug the stuff around with me all day, and some of the signs got ripped, and the balloons got wrecked.

"If you care so much, why didn't you call me last night to see where I was?"

"Because I'm grounded from the phone. And the computer. And going out."

Mel frowns. "How come?"

"It's such a mess," I say. "My mom came home the other night when I was supposed to be babysitting Katie and Luke was over. She flipped out and grounded me from everything. Which is ridiculous, because it wasn't even my fault. I had no idea he was going to come over." Suddenly I realize how much I've missed Mel. I don't have to talk in my Devi voice when I'm around Mel. I don't have to pretend to be a certain way, or to think about what lie I've told before I say anything. I can just be myself. "Mel, I really miss you," I say. "And I'm so sorry if I've been neglecting our friendship lately." I feel my voice catch, and suddenly my stomach drops.

This is the part where Mel's supposed to understand, wrap her arms around me in a huge hug, and then we walk off down the hall together, whispering and catching up. That's what happens in movies, anyway. And then the credits will come—that's how the movie ends, before anything bad can happen again, the one perfect moment that convinces the audience that everything is okay and is going to stay that way.

Instead, Mel slams her locker door shut and turns to look at me. "How come you never told me the real reason you went to stay with your grandma this summer?"

My heart stops. My face gets hot, and my head feels like it's spinning. "What?" I say.

"The real reason you went away for the summer," Mel says, and crosses her arms in front of her.

"What do you mean?" I croak.

"Just what I said." She looks at me, her blue eyes serious. "How come you never told me you went away because your parents were thinking about getting a divorce?"

"They weren't thinking about getting a divorce," I say. I don't know why I say that. It's a lie, and I can tell Mel knows it. But it's my first instinct. Oh. My. God. Have I become such a horrible person that my first instinct is *to lie*?

"Devon, please," she says. "My mom ran into your grandmother at the outlet malls and she told her all about it."

I don't say anything.

"Why didn't you tell me?" she asks again.

"I don't know," I say. It's not like she would have judged me or taken pity on me. She would have listened to me. Because she's a good friend. Unlike me, who's been horrible to her lately.

"Does Lexi know?" Mel demands.

"About my parents?"

"Yeah."

I don't say anything. Because Lexi does know.

"Yeah, that's what I thought," Mel says. Suddenly I'm scared. I start to realize that Mel is really, really angry at me. So angry that she might end our friendship. I take a deep breath.

"Mel, it wasn't like that," I say, trying to make sure my voice stays calm. "It wasn't like I told Lexi and didn't tell you. It was just easier to tell her."

"Because you trust her more," Mel says quietly.

"No!" I say. "Because I wasn't really friends with her, not the way I am with you." I shake my head vehemently. "Because she didn't really know me, and I didn't think I was ever going to see her again."

"And not because you guys are better friends?"

"No," I say, shaking my head. "Absolutely not."

Mel bites her lip, and for a second I think I may have won her over. But then Lexi picks that moment to come over and say good morning.

"Devi!" she squeals, coming up behind me and throwing her arms around me. "I feel so much better than yesterday!" I turn around. She's wearing the same sweater and belt as I am, and our hair is cut and colored the same way. "Hi, Mel!" Lexi says. "Are you okay? You weren't in school yesterday." Mel looks wordlessly between me and Lexi, then turns on her heel and walks away.

"You were wrong," Jared says, shrugging his shoulders. "Just admit it." He's turned around in his seat before the bell rings in English and he's giving me a headache. Of all the times I wished that Jared Bentley would turn around and start talking to me in English, would acknowledge my presence, even, this is never the way I imagined it.

"I wasn't wrong," I say, sighing. Which is true. I wasn't wrong about Lexi liking guys who play hard to get. Because I never thought it in the first place. Just because I knowingly gave Jared wrong information doesn't mean that I was wrong.

"Yes, you were," Jared says. His rolls his blue eyes. "She likes me better when I'm nice to her. In fact, she admitted that at first she thought I was kind of a jerk." He smiles smugly.

"When did she say that?"

"Last night on IM," he says. Great. Apparently Lexi

and Jared are like BFFs now. Which means it's only a matter of time before he (a) asks her out or (b) she lets it slip that she knows we're going out. Or used to go out. Whatever it is we're doing. "So you were wrong," Jared says again.

"Whatever, fine, I was wrong," I say miserably. Kim comes into the room wearing a light blue sweat suit that probably cost more than my parents' car. She sits down next to me and flips her hair back.

"Can you believe that thing with Kim and Matt?" Jared asks, lowering his voice. Jared, I've noticed, has become quite the gossip.

"Yeah, totally ridiculous," I say.

"I expected it from him, but her? That's so diabolical." I think Jared needs to work on his vocabulary. One should only use the word "diabolical" so many times before moving on to something else. "Calculating"? "Manipulative"? Both are acceptable choices.

At lunch I push a glop of chocolate pudding around my plate forlornly. Mel's sitting at our old table, the one we always used to sit at together until I had to start sitting with the A-list. I thought maybe at lunch I'd have a chance to smooth things over, but she doesn't even look at me.

"Hey," Luke says, sitting down next to me.

"Hi," I say. His chair is so close that our legs are almost touching. Not bare legs or anything, since obviously we're wearing pants, but still.

"So are you in a ton of trouble? I tried calling you yesterday, but your mom said you couldn't come to the phone." That was nice of her. To not tell people I was grounded, I mean.

"I'm grounded," I admit.

"That sucks," he says. "I'm really sorry. I feel like it was my fault. I shouldn't have shown up at your house like that."

"It's not your fault," I say. "I should have called my mom to let her know you had come over." God, his leg is really close to mine. If I move even a millimeter, we're probably going to be touching. I concentrate on keeping my leg perfectly still. Not that it would be horrible if our legs were touching or anything. I mean, people touch legs all the time. Right? Like in crowds and stuff. Or at sporting events. Plus we've already held hands. Leg touching is definitely a step down from that.

"I thought you were mad at me," he says, sounding relieved. "I tried to talk to you yesterday after social studies, but you took off pretty quickly."

"I was in a rush," I say lamely. I see Kim at the other end of the table, sitting next to Matt and sending me a death glare. What is her problem? Is it not enough that she has Matt and probably any other guys she might want? She has to stop every guy from hooking up with anyone besides her?

"You know, I tried to talk to your mom," he says. "I told her it was my fault, that I just showed up and you had no idea."

"You did?" How sweet.

"Yeah," he says. His leg shifts slightly. WE ARE TOUCHING LEGS. Our legs are touching. Ohmigod, ohmigod. I wonder if I should move it away. But then what if he thinks I don't want to be near him? But what if he's not touching my leg on purpose, or he doesn't realize what's going on, and then he moves his leg, and it's like he moved away first? And I'm the loser who wanted to touch legs with him while he didn't? And how come every time he's around, I end up worrying about STUFF LIKE THIS?

"Thanks for trying," I say. La, la, la. Ignoring the fact that we're touching legs.

"So listen," Luke says. He clears his throat. "About

what we were talking about the other day." He runs his fingers through his hair. His hair looks really cute today. Kind of spiky. Just enough gel so that it looks cute, but not greasy. I feel my face getting hot, and I quickly start flipping through the social studies notebook that's sitting next to my lunch tray, like I'm looking for some really crucial fact I have written down that's essential to our project.

"Yeah?" I say.

"So maybe this weekend after we finish our project, we can go to a movie or something. To celebrate."

I swallow. My first date, my first date, my first date.

"You mean like a date?" I ask, to clarify. Or to torture myself.

"Yes," he says. I glance down to the other end of the table, and I can tell Kim is listening to our every word. I can't go out with Luke. As much as I want to, I just can't.

"Listen, Luke," I say. "I think you're really cool and everything, but the truth is, my mom doesn't really allow me to date yet."

He looks away, but not before I catch the look of skepticism that crosses his face. A few seats down, I see Kim smirk. "No problem." I can tell he thinks I'm lying. Of course he thinks I'm lying! If that were true, why wouldn't I have just told him that from the beginning, instead of basically avoiding him?

"I'm not lying," I lie. "I just didn't tell you before because I didn't want you to think I was a loser." I'm flipping through my notebook now at a rapid pace. For some reason, I feel like I'm going to cry.

"It's not a big deal," he says. He starts getting his stuff together, getting ready to throw his tray away since the bell's about to ring. I feel desperate, like I need to say something before the bell rings. He stands up.

"Luke," I start. I look up at him. He's looking back down at me, a stricken look on his face. "What is it?" I ask, frowning.

I follow his gaze down to my notebook, where at the top of a page of social studies notes, there's a huge inked heart that says, DEVON LOVES JARED FOREVER. I drew it there one time during lunch in an effort to convince Lexi that I did, in fact, love Jared forever, and that he loved me. I meant to cross it out later.

"Luke . . . ," I say. "Listen, it isn't—"

"No, it's not a big deal," he says, shrugging. "You don't have to explain."

And for the second time that day, someone I care about turns around and walks away from me.

By the time school's over, I feel like I've been through a battle zone. I can't wait to get home, change into comfortable clothes, and watch DVDs. Although it might be nice to talk to my mom about some of the stuff that's going on. Maybe I can tell her everything: the lies, the fake boyfriend, the fact that Mel is mad at me because I didn't tell her about the stuff that was going on this summer. My mom is usually pretty good at listening. Maybe she'll have some advice.

I feel a little better, imagining my mom and I having one of those really nice moments you sometimes see on TV shows, where the girl and her mom have this heart-to-heart talk. But when I get home, my mom's sitting at the kitchen table, working on her laptop.

"What's for dinner?" I say, sitting myself down across from her. Maybe we'll even make tea. People in movies are always drinking tea during heart-to-heart chats. Or maybe hot chocolate. With marsh-mallows. "Do we have any hot chocolate?" I ask. I hop back up from my chair and start going through the cupboard over the microwave. Stuffing mix, a bottle of barbecue sauce, some soup. Where is the hot chocolate when I need it? I finally spot it behind some Cheez Doodles. I grab those too. I think I've earned the junk food.

"We're ordering pizza for dinner," my mom says.

I pull two mugs down from the shelf and dump a packet of hot chocolate into each of them. That definitely doesn't look like enough chocolate. I dump an extra packet into one of the cups, figuring I'm going to need mine extra strength.

"I'm going to make hot chocolate for us," I report. "Do you want double chocolate, or single?" She doesn't answer me, so I turn around. And my mom's standing behind me, her hands on her hips, holding a piece of paper in her hand.

"What's that?" I ask.

"It's a receipt for a sweater and a belt from bebe," she says.

"Oh," I say. "You can throw that out. They fit. I'm keeping them."

"It's dated for a time and date that you were supposed to be at school, making up a test."

"Oh." I am in so much trouble. I am in so much trouble, it's not even funny. I will not be allowed to leave the house until I'm thirty. I take a deep breath. "Mom," I say, "I can explain."

"Devon," she says. "Please go to your room."

chapter **eleven**

I didn't even get to have my extra chocolate hot chocolate. I had to go right to my room. And my mom had put a password on my computer, because I'm grounded from it, so all I could do was sit there and think about what a mess everything was. And how even my mom was mad at me. Aren't parents supposed to love you unconditionally? I threw myself on my bed and cried for a while, and then I decided it was time to do damage control. Real damage control this time. No more messing around.

The next morning I arrive at school early and

decorate Mel's locker with my HAPPY BFF DAY signs. I tape streamers to the outside of her locker. I put balloons up. I paste signs and stickers all over the place. And when she gets to school, instead of being excited, she takes one look at it and says, "What's this?"

"It's Happy BFF day!" I exclaim. "I know things have been weird between us lately, and I just wanted to tell you I'm sorry."

Mel looks at me. Then looks at her locker. Then looks at me again. She pushes some balloons out of the way and silently starts spinning her combination dial. I try another tactic. "So, listen, I'm technically grounded, but do you want to go to the library at lunch? Just the two of us? We could hang out and eat, catch up on everything that's been going on the past couple weeks."

"You think it's that easy, Devon?" She shakes her head. "You think you can just throw some balloons on my locker and that everything will be okay?" She slams her locker shut.

"No," I say. "I don't. But I just thought that if we could just sit down and talk, we could work it out. I just—"

"You kept a really big secret from me, Devon. And

we were supposed to be best friends. How would you feel if I did that to you?"

I feel my good mood evaporate. She's right. If Mel had kept something as big as her parents almost getting divorced from me, I would be really upset. "I wouldn't have liked it," I say.

"No," she says quietly. "You wouldn't have. And balloons and stuff don't really make up for that. But thanks."

"Devi!" Lexi calls, rushing up to me. Oh, God. Could she have picked a worse time? "I am having the worst morning." Her hair is a mess, and her eyes look like she's been crying. Yeah, join the club, I think.

"What is it? What's wrong?"

"It's Kim and Matt," she says, biting her lip. She glances at Mel, and I can tell she doesn't want Mel to know what's going on.

"Listen, Lexi," I say, taking a deep breath. "Can we talk about this in a little bit? I'll meet you at your locker in one minute. I was just trying to—"

"No, it's okay," Mel says. "I was just leaving." And she walks off down the hall. Crap.

"Devi," Lexi repeats. "Kim's telling everyone that I knew she liked Matt and I decided to go after him, anyway."

"That's insane," I say. "I am so sick of Kim and her crap. Besides, I thought she liked Luke." Saying his name out loud makes me feel weird. I think of the look on his face yesterday when he saw what was written in my notebook, and my stomach flips.

"I *never* knew she liked Matt," Lexi says.

"I know you didn't," I say, fuming. "And she knew YOU liked Matt and SHE went after him. It was completely the other way around."

"That's what Jared said!" Lexi says. She rummages through her bag and pulls out a Kleenex. She starts to dab her eyes.

"That's what Jared said?"

"Yeah, he said that's what Kim does. That she tries to turn things around on people." Lexi sighs. "But don't worry, Devi, there's nothing going on with Jared and me, I swear. We've just been talking a lot on IM, because he knows Kim and Matt really well." She sniffs again. "He's really a lot nicer than I thought. I can see why you liked him so much."

Oh, God. Can things get any worse? Now I'm apparently keeping Lexi away from her true love, when in actuality, I really couldn't care less if she dated Jared. Jared and his *Star Wars* book covers and weird hair-gel routines. I wish I had gotten to know him last year. I never would have liked him as much, and this whole mess could have been avoided.

"I just don't know what I'm going to do," Lexi says.

Kim comes walking down the hall then, holding Matt O'Connor's hand. She's wearing the shortest skirt I've ever seen someone wear when it's fifty degrees out. She looks like she just got her hair cut.

"What's up, Lexi?" she says, stopping to say hi like they're not fighting. I move closer to Lexi just in case Kim tries to start something. I've never been in a fight before, but I figure if I can channel my stress into fighting, I might have a good chance of winning.

"Nothing," Lexi says, her eyes narrowing. Matt looks at Lexi uncomfortably, kisses Kim's cheek, and then walks away down the hall.

"So, listen, I was thinking we could hang out after school," Kim says. "Matt has soccer practice with Jared"—she flicks her eyes toward me—"so maybe you can come over."

"Are you kidding?" Lexi says. She laughs. "You stole my boyfriend and you think you can just come over here and pretend like NOTHING'S WRONG?"

"Oh, please," Kim says, laughing. She tosses her hair over her shoulder. "He wasn't your boyfriend."

"Close enough," I say, feeling like I have to defend

my friend. Although Lexi doesn't seem like she needs any defending right now. She's not all sniffly and crying anymore. In fact, she looks really, really mad.

"Yeah, I guess according to you, that *would* be close enough, wouldn't it?" Kim scoffs. She rolls her eyes and tosses her hair behind her shoulder.

"Leave her out of this," Lexi says, too mad to even ask what Kim means by that. Thank God. "This is between me and you." Lexi's fists are clenched by her side. Wow. She's really mad. Instead of having Lexi's back, am I going to have to pull her off Kim? Are they going to fight?

"This is so ridiculous," Kim says. "You weren't even going out with him. He wasn't even yours." She studies her nails. "You're going to have to get a thicker skin than that, Lexi. Now can we please get over this whole little thing and talk about hanging out after school? Like I said, Matt has practice, but I'm sure we could get Luke and Jared to hang out."

I swallow. Lexi takes a step closer to Kim, and I put my hand out. "Lexi," I say. "Don't. She's not worth it."

"I'll decide if it's worth it or not," Lexi says. She takes another step toward Kim, and Kim moves back.

"You're not even serious," Kim says, starting to look a little scared. Not that I blame her. Lexi looks super mad, and she's at least twenty pounds heavier than Kim. I'm not even sure I could stop her if it came to that.

"Oh, I am serious," Lexi says. "Serious as a heart attack." Which is definitely not the coolest or scariest thing she could say in this situation, but I'm sure she's not thinking straight. With her impending fight and all.

"Lexi," I say, "Come on."

"Devi, stay out of it," Lexi instructs.

"Yeah, Devi," Kim says sweetly. "Stay out of it. Although . . ." she says slowly, raising her eyebrows. She grins. A horrible feeling starts in my stomach and moves through my body. "If you want to be mad at anyone, Lexi, you should be mad at Devi. Or Devon. Whatever."

"What do you mean?" Lexi asks, looking confused. "Why would I be mad at Devon?"

"Well," Kim says. "You seem to be super mad at me for going out with a guy who wasn't even yours in the first place, and yet Devon's the one who's been lying to you since you guys met."

"What do you mean?" Lexi asks, her voice sounding small. Some of the fire has definitely gone out of her. Her fists unclench, and she glances between Kim and me uncertainly.

"Kim . . . ," I start, trying to get my voice back.

"Hmm, where should I start?" Kim asks. She puts her finger on her chin and tilts her head to the side, like she really is considering. "Let's see . . ."

"Lexi," I say frantically. I grab her arm. "Come on, you don't have to listen to this. Let's get out of here." She shakes me off.

"Well, we should start with the fact that Devon said her name is Devi, which I've never heard anyone call her." She frowns and crinkles her eyes as if she's considering again. "Although, I wouldn't really know if that was true, since I never even knew her until you got here."

"What do you mean?" Lexi asks, frowning. She looks at me. "Devi, what does she mean?"

"Um, I dunno," I say brilliantly. DONOTPANIC, DONOTPANIC, DONOTPANIC. "I think she's just trying to cause trouble. Now, come on," I say to Lexi. "We don't have to listen to this." I'm totally in denial. I'm like one of those women on soap operas who finds the phone number of another woman in her husband's pocket and yet still doesn't think her husband is cheating.

"Not to mention the fact that she was never even dating Jared," Kim says.

"Devi?" Lexi says, looking at me. The look on her face is a mixture of confusion and awe.

"I have no idea what she's talking about," I say, laughing. "Ha-ha, good one, Kim." I look at Lexi, desperate. "She's just trying to cause trouble."

Kim rolls her eyes. "Devon, give it up." She looks down the hall to where Jared is standing with Luke, in front of Luke's locker.

"Hey, Jared," she calls. "Have you ever dated Devi?"

"No," Jared says. "Why?"

"See?" Kim says, ignoring him and turning back around.

"But . . . but she didn't tell anyone because Melissa likes him," Lexi says. But even as she's saying it, I can tell she knows the truth.

"That's just what she said so you wouldn't tell anyone," Kim says. "Now can we please talk about hanging out tonight?"

"No," Lexi says, taking a step back. She looks at me, and now she looks really upset. "We can't."

The rest of the day is a nightmare. I huddle in the library during lunch, pretending to be engrossed in a book that I've plucked randomly off the shelf. But all I can think about is the fact that everyone hates me. I consider pretending to be sick and going to the nurse's office, but then I figure if Kim notices I'm not in English, it might just be worse. When I do get to English, Kim and Jared ignore me. Which leaves me grateful, as there's no way I wanted to deal with anyone taunting me. In social studies, Luke ignores me too.

When I get home from school, my mom's in the living room, having a cup of tea and watching *Oprah*.

"Hi," she says.

"Hi." I plop myself down on the couch. I'm so emotionally exhausted that I think I might have to sleep for a year.

"There are chocolate chip cookies in the kitchen if you want some," she says. "I finished a huge project today, so I had some time on my hands."

I burst into tears.

"Oh my goodness, Devon, what's wrong?" My mom sits up in the chair she's in and sets her mug down on the coffee table.

"Everything," I say. And everything is wrong. Even my mom, who I've obviously disappointed by lying to her and being the worst daughter ever, is making me cookies. Cookies that I don't deserve.

"Tell me," she says. And so I do. The whole thing.

From the beginning. How I lied this summer about Jared being my boyfriend. How Lexi showed up at school. How I started to like Luke. How I never told Mel about the problems my parents were having. How Jared and Lexi like each other, but aren't together because of me. How Kim told everyone. How I feel horrible for lying to her and sneaking out while I was grounded.

"And the thing is," I say, when I finish, "is that I don't know how to fix any of it. It's like things just keep getting worse and worse. And the most horrible part is that it's all my fault." My mom hands me a tissue. I blow my nose. "I'm a horrible person, and I deserve everything I get."

"Oh, Devon," my mom says. "You're not a horrible person. You just got caught up in a bad situation."

"A bad situation that I started," I say, sniffling.

"People make mistakes," my mom says, shrugging. "I don't think you did any of this knowing you were going to hurt people, did you?"

"No," I say. "But the point is that I did hurt people. I hurt everyone. Everyone I cared about, or who trusted me."

"So fix it," my mom says. "It's not about if you screwed up or not. Everyone screws up. It's how you fix it that counts."

"But how?" I say. "How do I fix it?"

"You have to tell the truth," my mom says.

"But they already all know the truth."

"No, they don't," my mom points out. "And the truth they do know, they heard from someone else. They need to hear it from you. They have to hear you take responsibility for what you did."

She heads to the kitchen and comes back with two steaming mugs of tea and a plateful of cookies. Why is it that the hardest thing and the right thing are always the same?

On Saturday I'm supposed to go to Jared's to finish filming our project, which means I can't avoid the inevitable anymore. I haven't talked to Luke or anyone about the plan, so I call him on Saturday morning to make sure we're still on.

"Um, hi," I say when he answers the phone. "It's Devon."

"Yeah?" he says. He sounds like he could care less it's me, which scares me a little bit. At least if he's mad at me, it means he cares a little, right? I take a deep breath.

"Uh, I was just calling to make sure we're still on for today," I say. Great. The way I said that makes it out like we're going out on a date or something. "I mean, is everyone still going to film the project?"

"Yes," he says. Silence. I almost want to ask him if I'm still invited, but that's crazy, right? I mean, it's MY project too. They couldn't disinvite me even if they wanted to. "Is that all?"

"Oh, okay," I say, trying to sound breezy. There's a lump in my throat, though, so my words come out kind of strangled.

Silence again on the phone. It goes on so long that I'm not sure Luke is still even there. Should I just hang up? Say bye? "Um, are you still there?" I ask. Silence. "Hello?"

"Yeah, I'm here," he says.

"Oh. You weren't saying anything."

"I said 'Is that all?'"

"That was like five minutes ago." Silence again. I don't want him to hang up the phone. "Listen, I don't want things to be weird between us," I say.

"Okay."

"Luke—"

"I don't want things to be weird either." He sighs.

"Good, because with the project and everything—"

"I know you like Jared, enough to make up the fact that he was your boyfriend. Kim told me."

"Luke, I—"

"No, it's not a big deal. I just wanted you to know that you could have told me you weren't interested in hanging out, that you liked someone else. You didn't have to lie, Devon." He pauses. "But I guess that's what you do. Lie, I mean."

"No!" I say. "I mean, yes, I do lie. I mean, I did lie, but I don't like Jared, Luke. I never liked Jared. Well, I mean, I did like Jared, but I don't know, it was just—"

"Whatever," he says, cutting me off. "I said what I wanted to say. We still have a little bit of work to do on our project, and I don't want our grade to suffer just because things are weird between you and me."

And then he really does hang up, because there's a dial tone in my ear, and I set the receiver back down.

I feel the burning start behind my eyes, hot pinpricks that will turn into tears.

"What's wrong, Devon?" Katie asks. She comes into the kitchen from the living room, wearing a pair of footie pajamas. Her hair is in a messy ponytail.

"I'm sad," I say.

"How come?" I sit down at the table, and she crawls up onto my lap and rests her head on my shoulder.

"Because a lot of people are mad at me," I say.

"Did you do something bad?" Katie asks knowingly.

"Yes," I say. "I did."

"Then say you're sorry," Katie says. "And they will forgive you." She wraps a strand of my hair around her finger.

"But what if they don't?" I say.

"Of course they will," Katie says, rolling her eyes. "If you did something bad to me, and then you said sorry, I would forgive you."

"You would?"

"Of course." She hops down from my lap. "Wanna make Rice Krispies Treats?"

"Sure," I say, wiping my tears with a napkin on the table. And so we do.

Three hours and three batches of Rice Krispies Treats later (we were trying to get the marshmallow-to-Rice Krispies ratio just right, which involved sending my dad to the grocery store for more marshmallows at one point, since we were using bags upon bags), I'm standing at Jared's front door.

I've decided to look at this like I'm a soldier going off to battle, just something that I need to get through in order to get on with my life. I ring the doorbell.

Jared answers the door. "Whaddup?" he says when he sees me standing there.

"Um, nothing," I say.

"We're downstairs." He turns around, and I follow him through his living room and to the basement door. He doesn't seem mad at me, which is a good sign. But I've spoken too soon, because once I'm downstairs, it becomes apparent that this is going to be a lot harder than I thought.

No one says hi to me. For the first ten minutes, while Matt's setting up the camera and everyone else is talking and eating snacks, I sit on the couch, saying and doing nothing.

Finally Lexi comes up to me, holding a black robe and white wig. "Here," she says. "This is your costume."

"Thanks," I say, taking it. "Uh, where should I change?"

"You can just put it on over your clothes," she says, taking in my blue sweater and jeans. I slip the robe on and put the white wig over my hair. There are no mirrors in Jared's basement, and I hope I don't look too goofy.

"This is crazy," Kim is saying. "Luke, can we please not wear this stuff?" She looks at the robe with disdain.

"What do you think they wore back then, Kim?" Jared asks, rolling his eyes.

"Well, they should have worn stuff that was cuter.

Maybe they would have lived longer." She giggles and puts her hand on her hip, showing off the tight pink T-shirt she's wearing. I think Kim stuffs her bra.

I look over to where Matt is setting up the camera, wondering how he's going to react to Kim flirting with Jared, but he doesn't seem to notice.

"Can I at least go upstairs and look in the mirror?" Kim asks, rummaging through her purse and pulling out a lip gloss and a compact. "Plus I'm going to need more makeup if I'm going to be filmed."

"Fine," Jared says.

"Lexi, wanna come with?" Kim asks, but Lexi just shakes her head.

Kim bounds up the stairs.

"Okay," Matt says. "The camera's ready." He holds it on his shoulder, and starts filming. "This," he says, "is Jared." He zooms in on Jared, who looks annoyed and puts his hand up.

Kim returns, looking cute in her wig and her robe. "I'm ready," she sings, doing a little twirl.

It doesn't take the long to film the project. Except for a few small mix-ups, everyone seems to know their lines pretty well. Even Jared.

"Hey, Luke," Kim says when we're finished filming, folding up her robe and placing it in the plastic bag on

Jared's sofa. "What are you doing after this? You want to come over?"

I start pulling off my own robe, pretending I'm not listening, but I'm secretly pleased when Luke replies, "I can't," and doesn't offer any other explanation.

"Hey, Lexi," I say on our way out. "Can I talk to you for a second?"

"Nope," she says, and then marches up the stairs. When we get outside, she hops into her mom's van, and it might be my imagination, but I think I catch her mom giving me a dirty look before they pull out and get onto the road. All right then.

When I get home, I make the following list:

Problems, Reasons, and Possible Solutions

Problem Number One: Mel is mad at me.

Reason: I basically blew her off while I pretended to be Devi, and I didn't tell her about my parents.

Possible Solution: Beg for Mel's forgiveness? Explain to her exactly what is going on with my parents and why I didn't want to tell her. Apologize.

Problem Number Two: Lexi is mad at me.

Reason: I lied to her about basically everything.

Possible Solution: Tell her why I lied—that it felt good being able to be someone else for a while, and that just because I lied about certain aspects of my life doesn't mean that our friendship wasn't real. Tell Jared to stop being mean to Lexi. Apologize.

Problem Number Three: Luke is mad at me.

Reason: He thinks I led him on, when I really liked Jared.

Possible Solution: Tell Luke the truth, that I did used to like Jared, but I don't anymore. Tell Luke I like him. Make him listen if he doesn't want to. Apologize.

BOTTOM LINE: I have a lot of work to do, and it isn't going to be easy.

On Monday morning I march up to Jared's locker even though he's standing there with Luke. At this point, I have nothing to lose. Plus I figure if I was able to do this kind of stuff when I was Devi, I should certainly be able to do it now, when it's much more important.

"Hey," I say.

"Hey," Jared says. Luke looks at the ground uncomfortably.

"I need to talk to you," I say.

"It's almost time for homeroom," Jared says. He slams his locker door shut.

"Yeah, I know," I say. "But I need to tell you something."

"Okay," he says, shrugging.

"I'll catch you later," Luke says to Jared, but as Jared and I walk down the hall, I can feel Luke's eyes boring holes into my back. My heart leaps a little bit. If he's interested at least a little bit in what's going on between Jared and me, he must still care, right?

"So listen," I say, taking a deep breath. This is going to be tough. "I know you know that I lied about you being my boyfriend."

"Yup," Jared says, nodding. He shifts his books from one arm to the other.

"Are you mad?" I frown.

"Not really," he says, shrugging. "It's pretty obvious that you had a crush on me."

"It is? I mean, it was?" This is not the way things are supposed to go down. Even though he seemed cool at his house on Saturday, I expected him to be a little angrier at me.

"Yeah."

"Yeah, well, I did have a crush on you last year," I say. "But I don't now." He doesn't say anything, so I take a deep breath. "And I'm sorry, because I made it really difficult for you to get to know Lexi better. I told you to be mean to her, and that was wrong of me."

"Yeah, I kind of figured that out," he says. "But it doesn't really matter now. She likes Matt."

"No," I say. "She doesn't."

"She doesn't? But she's always talking about him, about how mad she is that he's with Kim now."

"Yeah, she's mad that he was a jerk to her, but I really think she's over it." I lean in closer to Jared and lower my voice. "In fact, the last few times we've hung out, all she can talk about is how great you've been to her."

"Really?" he says, his eyes lighting up.

"Yeah," I say. "And I think the only reason she didn't seem interested in you before was because she thought I liked you. Which I don't. Anymore."

"So what should I do?" he asks.

"Ask her out. Be nice to her."

"You think she'll go for it?"

"Yeah," I say. "I do.

"Thanks, Devi." The bell rings then, and he heads off to homeroom. One down, three more to go.

In social studies, I approach Luke before the bell rings.

"Hey," I say. "Do you think I could talk to you for a second?"

"If you're worried about the project, I have it," he says, holding up the DVD of our skit.

"Um, no," I say, "that's not what I wanted to talk to you about."

"Then no," he says, "I don't want to talk."

"Luke, listen," I say. "I did like Jared, and I did lie to Lexi about going out with him. But that was before I knew him, before I knew you." I swallow and look down at my hands. "And I'm sorry if I hurt your feelings, and I'm sorry that I lied."

"Is that all?" he says, looking straight ahead.

"Yeah," I say. "I guess so." This is all wrong. This is not how this is supposed to be happening. Luke is supposed to forgive me, to tell me it's okay, that he doesn't have any hard feelings. Isn't that what happens when people apologize? Suddenly I realize that people may not want to forgive me. That maybe I've done irreparable damage.

"Well, thanks," he says. "I appreciate you apologizing."

He turns around, toward the front of the classroom, and I have no choice but to head to my seat.

❂ ❂ ❂

For the second day in a row, I drag myself home, dejected.

"Whaddup?" Katie asks happily when she sees me. She's wearing a snowsuit and a pair of swim goggles.

"I'm upset," I declare, walking into the living room and throwing myself down on the couch.

Katie follows me. "I'm a skier," she says happily.

"Great," I say.

"Devon! Cheer up!" she demands.

"I can't," I say.

"Why not?" She pulls her goggles off her eyes.

"Because I'm still sad," I say.

"Did you apologize?" she asks.

"Yes," I say.

She frowns and puts her hands on her hips. "Did you really apologize? Did you try your very hardest?"

"Well . . ." I didn't, really. I haven't even talked to Mel or Lexi yet, although the way things are going, I'm not in a rush to do so.

"Then you must not admit defeat," Katie says solemnly. "You need to have the heart of a champion." She snaps her goggles back over her eyes and pretends to be skiing down a mountain. I start laughing. I can't help it. She just looks so funny, talking like a five-year-old philosopher, and dressed in a ski outfit.

"I love you, Katie Kate," I say.

"I love you, too, Devi Dev," she says.

"Hey," I say. "You want to ask Mom and Dad if we can go out to dinner tonight?"

"Yeah!" she says, then frowns. "Can I wear my ski outfit?"

"Well, duh," I say, rolling my eyes. "Of course."

My parents agree to take us out to dinner at a steakhouse in the mall. We order steaks and big gooey desserts, and my mom tells a story about my dad getting chased all over the lawn by a squirrel this summer while Katie and I were at my grandma's. After dinner, we even take my parents to DDR. Surprisingly my mom is really good at it. It feels nice. Although I see Matt O'Connor at the arcade with Kayleigh Trusco, I'm able to ignore them, and just be with my family, laughing and having fun. For a while, I forget about the stuff that's going on with Mel, with Lexi, with Luke, with everyone. But then, as we're leaving the arcade, something happens that brings it all back.

On the way out, I run into Brent Madison, the guy Mel's had a crush on forever.

"Hey," he says when he sees me. "Where's your other half?"

"My other half?" I ask.

"Yeah, cute girl with blue eyes? Really tiny?" He holds his hand up to indicate a short person. I stare at him blankly. "Melissa?" he says, probably thinking I'm an idiot.

"Oh," I say, laughing. "She's not here."

"Well, tell her I miss you guys giggling in the library and distracting me from my work." He turns around then and heads into the restaurant, and I feel a surge of elation pass through me. He asked about Mel!

But just like that, it disappears. Mel's not talking to me, so it's not like I can tell her.

"Hey, Mom?" I ask in the car on the way home. "Can you take me to Mel's?"

"Now?" my mom asks.

"Yeah," I say, holding my breath. She glances at my dad. "It's a school night."

"Yeah, I know," I say.

She looks at me in the rearview mirror, and for a second, I think she's going to point out the fact that I'm grounded. But she doesn't. She just nods. We drop my sister and my dad at home first, and then take the car over to Mel's.

@ @ @

My stomach starts to churn nervously. I didn't call her to tell her I was coming, figuring it would probably be better to just show up. She probably would have said she didn't want to see me, and I don't want to have to do this over the phone.

We pull into Mel's driveway, and my mom puts the car in park. "Wait," I say. "I don't know if I can do this."

"Sure you can," my mom says.

"I don't think so," I say, shaking my head. "She's going to hate me. She's going to be really mad at me."

"She's already really mad at you," my mom points out. "At this point, you have nothing to lose."

She's right. I open the car door slowly. I feel like that movie, *Dead Man Walking*. Only I'm like dead teenager walking or something. Not that this situation is the same as being on death row or anything. But it's still pretty bad.

I ring the doorbell and stand on the porch, waiting for someone to answer the door. Both of Mel's parents' cars are here, so I know they're home. What if Mel slams the door in my face? Or what if she makes one of her parents come to the door to tell me she's not home? Or what if—

"Oh," Mel says, opening the door. "It's you."

"Yeah," I say. "It's me." There's an awkward silence. She doesn't invite me in. Why isn't she inviting me in? Oh, right. Because she's mad at me for being a terrible friend. "Um, can I come in?"

"I guess so," she says, shrugging. She walks away from the door. I guess I'm supposed to follow her. I glance over my shoulder. My mom gives me a reassuring little wave from the car.

"So," I say, once we're sitting in Mel's living room. It feels weird being here, in her living room. Usually when I come over, we head right to her room. Being in the living room doesn't feel right, like I'm a stranger or someone who she doesn't feel comfortable letting into her bedroom.

"So," Mel says. She stretches herself out on the couch. She looks bored.

"How have you been?"

"Fine." I had this whole thing planned out, how I was going to confess everything and apologize, and now that I'm here, it's like the words won't come. I realize how devastated I'm going to be if I lose Mel's friendship.

"Good," I say. I take a deep breath. "Listen, I'm so sorry. About everything." When in doubt, start with an apology.

"It's okay," she says, shrugging. "It's not a big deal." But she doesn't mean it, I can tell.

"It *is* a big deal," I say. "At least to me." I sigh. "Mel, I'm so sorry I didn't tell you about my parents. But it was this whole weird thing. I mean, we were supposed to be going away to stay with my grandma in case my parents got divorced." I look down at the couch. "And it was just easier for me not to deal with it, you know?"

"But you told Lexi," Mel says quietly. "You told Lexi, and you didn't tell me."

"I know," I say. "And I know you think it's because I think Lexi's a better friend, or because I trust her more. But that's not why." I feel my voice start to catch, so I rush on. "Lexi didn't know me the way you do, Mel. Lexi thought I was this totally cool, totally together person who had a hot boyfriend and could deal with things like her parents getting divorced. I knew she wouldn't feel sorry for me." Mel looks at me, and I keep going. "But I knew you would know how hard it was going to be for me if my parents were going to get a divorce. And I didn't really want to talk about it or think about it." I feel the tears pricking the back of my eyelids. "I'm so, so sorry Mel."

"I'm sorry too," she says. "I had no idea. I should have figured it would be hard for you."

"I never meant to keep secrets from you, or hide something from you," I say. I'm crying now, and Mel grabs a tissue off the coffee table and hands it to me.

"How are they now?" she asks. "Your parents, I mean?"

"They're good," I say, wiping my nose. "Well, they're doing better. My mom got all her job stuff worked out, and they're going to a counselor. They seem happier."

"That's good," Mel says. She sighs. "And I'm sorry if I've been overreacting to you hanging out with Lexi so much. I just felt really left out."

"I know," I say. "And that's going to stop."

"You're allowed to have other friends, Devon," she says.

"I know," I say. "I know I am. But that doesn't mean I have to neglect you at the same time."

"Hey, do you want to hang out for a while? We could watch a movie. Maybe eat ice cream or something?" She looks hopeful.

"I'd love to," I say. "But I'm grounded."

"Oh," Mel says, her face falling.

"But maybe . . ." I run outside, have a quick conference with my mom, and then run back inside. "You have me for a whole hour," I say happily. "And you will never guess what happened tonight."

I fill Mel in on the whole Brent story, and we spend the rest of the hour obsessing over what she should do. It feels really nice to have my friend back. And for her to know the truth.

"You have to talk to him," I say to Mel, slamming my locker door shut the next morning. Our debate from last night has carried over, because Mel is acting like a wimp.

"I can't!" she gasps, looking terrified. "What would I say?"

"I dunno," I say. "Something about the assignment? Yeah, ask him about the math assignment."

"Ya think?" She bites her lip.

"Totally." We start to walk toward our homerooms when Lexi stops me.

"Hey," I say warily, not sure if I can handle another really bad encounter. I have Mel back, and I'm not sure if my brain can take any more drama right now.

"Hey," she says. "Listen, I know you talked to Jared for me." She bites her lip. "So thanks."

"No problem."

"We're going to hang out this weekend."

"That's great," I say honestly.

"Yeah . . ." she trails off, and then I realize she's waiting for me to give her permission. After everything I've done to her, she doesn't want to go out with him if she thinks I still like him. I feel the tears start in the back of my eyes. Mel squeezes my hand, which makes me feel better.

"Lexi, it's fine if you go out with Jared."

"Are you sure?" she asks, twirling a strand of her hair around her finger. "Because I know what it's like when someone goes out with the guy you like."

"It's fine."

"Okay," she hesitates, then starts walking away. I look at Mel, who squeezes my hand again.

"Lexi, wait," I say. She turns around. "I don't know how things got so screwed up." I can feel myself starting to tear up. "Lexi, I'm so, so, sorry." A tear slips down my cheek. "I'm really sorry. I never meant to lie to you. It was just that this summer, getting away from my parents and everything, I just . . . I don't know, I wanted to be someone else, I guess. And you've been such a good friend to me, and I just . . ."

Lexi sighs. "I just wish you had told me what was going on from the moment I got here."

"I know," I say. "I wanted to, but it was just really

hard. I understand if you don't ever want to talk to me again." She doesn't say anything, so I keep going. "But Lexi, our friendship is really important to me. That doesn't change just because I lied about a few details of my life."

Lexi bites her lip. "It's okay," she finally says, reaching out to hug me. "It's okay."

"But I lied to you," I say, still crying. I hope I'm not getting snot on her shirt. It looks expensive.

"Yeah, but you did it for a reason," she says, shrugging.

"You're not mad?" I ask, pulling away. I wipe my tears with the back of my hand.

"I was," she says, sighing. "But, Devi, I never liked you because you had a boyfriend. I mean, I didn't even know who Jared was until I got here. For all I knew, he could have been some disgusting, hairy guy with eight toes." She wrinkles her nose in disgust. I laugh.

"Hey, Lexi!" a voice yells behind us. We turn around and see Kim walking down the hall toward us.

"Oh, great," Lexi says. "It's the boyfriend-stealing blackmailer."

"What do you want?" I ask Kim, realizing I can be as mean to her as I want now that she can't hold anything over me. Then I realize that in order to tell my secret, Kim must have been fairly confident that Luke was so mad, he would never forgive me. I feel myself getting angrier. Three on one. We could definitely take her.

"I need my Seven jeans back," Kim says, tossing her hair over her shoulder. "You've had them for, like, a week."

"Fine," Lexi says. "Then I'll need my blue necklace."

"I don't have your blue necklace," Kim says, shrugging.

"Yes, you do," Lexi says.

"Well, I'll check, but I really don't think I do," Kim says sweetly. "I think I gave it back to you."

"You didn't," Lexi says.

"Well, I don't have it," Kim says again. "I might have left it at Matt's." She smiles viciously.

"Well, if that's the case, you can probably just ask Kayleigh Trusco to give it back to you," I say to Lexi, nodding.

"What's that supposed to mean?" Kim asks, glaring at me.

"Nothing," I say, looking innocent. "It's just that

last night I saw Matt at the arcade with Kayleigh Trusco, and it looked like they were having a lot of fun. So Lexi can probably just get Kayleigh to pick it up next time she's at his house."

Kim's eyes narrow, and she glares at all of us, then turns on her heel and marches down the hall. Lexi, Mel, and I burst out laughing.

chapter twelve

"You have to eat something," Mel says at lunch. We're in the caf at our own table—me, Mel, and Lexi. Although Lexi keeps getting up to go sit with Jared and the rest of the A-list (including Luke) periodically, and although she invited me and Mel to sit there, I didn't feel like dealing with it.

"Fine," I say. I pick up a french fry from my tray, drag it through some ketchup, and pop it into my mouth. "Are you happy?"

"Eat another one," Mel instructs. So I do.

"I don't understand why you won't just talk to

him," Lexi says. She pulls her mirror out of her purse and fluffs her hair.

"Because he won't listen to me," I say. "He hates me."

"He doesn't hate you," Lexi says, rolling her eyes.

"You just have to talk to him," Mel says.

"I already tried that," I say.

"But did you tell him you really, really like him?" Lexi asks.

"No," I admit.

"You have to," Mel says, and Lexi nods.

"But I've already humiliated myself enough," I wail.

"'And the trouble is, if you risk nothing, you risk even more,'" Lexi recites. Mel and I look at her in surprise. "What?" she says. "It's like a famous quote." I eat another fry. And another. "Hey, do you want to hang out after school today? I might be able to con my mom into letting you guys come over for a little while."

"Sure," Mel says. "But I have to work on my English while I'm over. Last week I got a C minus on my poetry quiz because—" She gets a weird look on her face, stops talking, and leans in close to me.

"What is it?" I ask. I pop another fry into my mouth.

"Don't freak out," she says, "but Luke is coming over here."

"What?" I say. I chew and swallow my fry quickly. "Are you sure? Why would he—"

"Hey," a voice says behind me, and I turn around. Luke. "Can I talk to you for a second?"

"Sure," I say, trying to keep my voice even. I look at Mel and Lexi, trying to have a conversation with them about what I should do without saying anything.

I follow him to just outside of the cafeteria doors, where we stand against the wall. "Listen, I wanted to let you know that the project is pretty much done. I'll give you the write-up in social studies so you can look it over, but I think it's in pretty good shape."

"Oh," I say. "Okay." So Luke did the rest of the project himself. I was kind of hoping that we'd work on it together, and he'd come around and realize how cool I am, and, you know, not hate me. I was also half-hoping that Luke wanted to talk to me about something important, like what was going on with us, instead of the stupid project. But I guess that was the last thing that would force us to have contact and now he just wants to be done with me. "Thanks for letting me know," I say, then turn around and start heading back toward the cafeteria.

"Devon," he says, grabbing my arm.

"Yeah?" I say, turning back around.

"Listen, I talked to Lexi this morning." He leans against the wall and sighs. "She told me that you had a crush on Jared last year, but that you never really liked him the way you like me. Is that true?"

"Yes," I say. "That's true."

"She told me how you came clean, told her the truth. And she also told me what Kim's been doing to you."

"Oh," I say.

"I'm sorry I was so hard on you on Saturday," he says. "It's just that I'd thought you kind of liked me, and I really liked you, and then I found out you liked Jared, and . . . I don't know, I was upset."

"But I don't like Jared." I say. My heart's beating really fast. I swallow, and then go for it. "I like you."

"I know that now," he says. "But I didn't at the time." He's moving closer to me now. Or maybe it's my imagination. No, it's really slow, but he's definitely moving closer to me. I can smell his Luke smell.

"I'm sorry I lied to you," I say. "I just—"

"It's okay," he says, putting a finger on my lips. And then he leans down and brushes his lips against mine. They're soft and salty, and I can feel his cheek brush against mine when he pulls away. Oh My God. Luke just kissed me. I've just been kissed! My first kiss!

"Oh," I say. That's all I can think to say. Just oh.

"Devi!" Lexi screams from behind me. "What is going on out here?" She's standing in the doorway of the cafeteria, her hands on her hips. "Ohmigod, you guys are kissing! I knew it! I knew you were going to get together! Mel was all, 'What is taking them so long,' and I was like, 'I'll bet they're getting together.'"

Mel pokes her head around Lexi. "Is everything okay?" she asks. "We just wanted to check on you."

"Yes," I say, laughing. "Everything's fine."

"Good," Mel says. "Come on, Lexi." She looks at me. "We're going back in the caf now. But, uh, call us if you need us."

"Yeah, call us if you need us," Lexi agrees, nodding. She looks a little disappointed, like she wants to keep spying on us, but Mel hustles her back into the cafeteria.

"They're nuts," I say, laughing.

"Nah," Luke says. "They're just worried about you."

"I know," I say. "But they don't need to be." And then I kiss Luke again, right there outside the cafeteria.

About the Author

Lauren Barnholdt was born and raised in Syracuse, New York, and now resides in central Connecticut. If you ask people who knew her in junior high, they may tell you she had a few secret identities of her own. She's the author of the YA novels *Reality Chick* and *Two-Way Street*, both available from Simon Pulse. When she's not writing, you can find her watching reality TV, playing DDR, or reading. Visit her website at www.laurenbarnholdt.com or her MySpace site at www.myspace.com/lauren_barnholdt.